The Jerry McNeal Series

Wicked Winds

(A Paranormal Snapshot)

By Sherry A. Burton

Also by Sherry A. Burton

The Orphan Train Saga

Discovery (book one)

Shameless (book two)

Treachery (book three)

Guardian (book four)

Loyal (book five)

Orphan Train Extras

Ezra's Story

Jerry McNeal Series

Always Faithful (book one)

Ghostly Guidance (book two)

Rambling Spirit (book three)

Chosen Path (book four)

Port Hope (book five)

Cold Case (book six)

Wicked Winds (book seven)

Mystic Angel (book eight)

Spirit of Deadwood

Romance Books*

Tears of Betrayal

Love in the Bluegrass

Somewhere In My Dreams

The King of My Heart

Seems Like Yesterday

"Whispers of the Past," a short story.

Psychological Thriller

Surviving the Storm

*A note from the author: With the exception of *Seems Like Yesterday* (which has been revised to be a clean read), my romance books have SEX. A couple of them have sex more than a few times. We are not talking close the door and turn off the lights sex. We are talking glow-in-the-dark condoms (*King of My Heart*). *Surviving the Storm* is a lot darker than my other titles and may not be for all readers. While I no longer write books where the lovemaking scenes are so detailed, I am not removing them from these early books, as the readers seem to enjoy them.

The Jerry McNeal Series

Wicked Winds

By Sherry A. Burton

The Jerry McNeal Series: Wicked Winds

by Sherry A. Burton
Published by Dorry Press
Edited and Formatted by BZHercules.com
Cover by Laura J. Prevost
@laurajprevostphotography
Proofread by Latisha Rich

ISBN 978-1-951386-24-5

For more information on the author and her works, please see www.SherryABurton.com

I will forever be grateful to my mom, who insisted the dog stay in the series.
To my hubby, thanks for helping me stay in the writing chair.
To my editor, Beth, for allowing me to keep my voice.
To Laura, for EVERYTHING you do to keep me current in both my covers and graphics.
To my beta readers for giving the books an early read.
To my proofreader, Latisha Rich, for the extra set of eyes.
To my fans, for the continued support.
Lastly, to my "writing voices," thank you for all the incredible ideas!

Table of Contents

Chapter One

For the fifth time in as many months, everything Jerry McNeal owned was loaded into the back of his Durango, and Gunter, his ghostly K-9 companion, sat in the passenger seat eagerly awaiting their next adventure. Jerry pulled out the paper Seltzer had given him and scanned it. Unnecessary, as Jerry could recite the names in his sleep.

Although all the women on the list were redheads, that did not mean they were victims of the Hash Mark Killer, but because they were redheads, he had a reason to look into their disappearances. He plucked a pen from the console, skimmed the list, and crossed off the name Rita Wadsworth – the woman he'd just found in Niagara Falls. Neither Patti O'Conner nor Ashley Fabel was on the list. It wasn't that they weren't connected – they weren't on the list because while their murders hadn't been solved, they were no longer missing. All thanks to the concerted effort of his psychic friend Max and ghostly partner Gunter.

Patti and Ashley had each been found sharing a shallow grave with a legal inhabitant. Furthermore, both victims had spoken with him beyond the grave, sharing intimate details of their deaths. Jerry knew the murders to be connected. The problem was he needed more than the word of a ghost to take his hunch to authorities.

Desperate for answers, Jerry had asked his former sergeant to use his resources at the Pennsylvania State Police Post to compile a list of women who'd fit their description – women with red hair who'd been reported missing without a trace in recent years.

Unfortunately, the inquiry had raised red flags and put both Jerry and Sergeant Seltzer on the radar of some people who were not very forthcoming about their own interest in the proceedings. Fred and Barney – obviously not the men's real names – were the least of their worries, as the next victim – a Ms. Rosie Freeman – disappeared in Salem, Massachusetts, much too close to the stomping ground of one Mario Fabel.

Fabel was the brother of Ashley Fabel, a woman who'd gone missing in Michigan in August 2019. While Fabel was relieved to learn the whereabouts of his sister's remains and exceedingly generous with the reward, the man was less than thrilled that Jerry hadn't satisfied his request to know how he had come to discover Ashley's whereabouts. Especially since the earth covering his sister's body had not been disturbed for several years. Jerry had little doubt that the sole reason Fabel hadn't leaned on him more was that Jerry was ready for him when he came. That and the fact Jerry had turned the sizable reward over to Max and her mother, April, without keeping any for himself.

It wasn't that Jerry was trying to throw Fabel off his trail. He hadn't done anything that needed covering. The simple truth of the matter, if not for Max's psychic abilities and the fact that Fabel's sister was haunting the girl, Jerry wouldn't have known the woman was missing in the first place. Max was the rightful recipient of the money, plain and simple.

That Fabel hadn't pressed Max or her mother for more information was the only reason Jerry hadn't seen the need to have any further dealings with the guy. The problem, while Jerry was finished with Fabel, he had no doubt that if the man discovered him to be heading his way, he would want to pick up where they'd left off. Only this time, Jerry would be on Fabel's turf, and the man had already shown he had a dark side. Jerry ran a hand through his hair, sighed, then scratched the K-9 behind the ear.

Gunter closed his eyes and leaned into Jerry's hand, his right leg lifting up and down as if it were he doing the scratching. Jerry continued to massage the dog's ear as he spoke. "Guess we'll head over to Salem to see if we can find Rosie Freeman. According to Sarge's information, she went missing while on summer break from Quincy College in Quincy, Massachusetts. She and some friends drove the short distance to Salem and rented a summer home for the weekend. Rosie stepped outside to have a cigarette and was never seen again."

Gunter opened his eyes, bared his teeth, and gave a menacing growl.

Jerry gave the dog a firm pat to let him know he was finished, then began plugging the address into the navigator. "Don't worry, boy; we're going to nail this guy."

***

Four hours into the trip, Jerry felt a crawling sensation on the back of his neck. It was too early to be a hit on the woman he was going to see, but something was up, as Gunter had disappeared from the passenger side and was currently on the second-row seat pacing from side to side.

Jerry ran his hand over his head to calm his nerves. It didn't work. He saw an exit ramp and decided to take it, thinking to stretch his legs and grab a bite to eat. He eased into the right lane, which emptied into the exit lane. The moment he did, he saw a temporary construction sign stating the reentry ramp was closed. He glanced over his shoulder, hoping to swing back into traffic, but his way was blocked by a semi that'd moved into the lane he'd just vacated. *Great!* Jerry sighed and continued down the off-ramp.

He looked at Gunter through the rearview mirror. "The sign said there's a restaurant. I'll grab a bite to eat, and we'll find another way around."

Gunter ignored his comment and continued to move from one side to the other.

Jerry stopped at the stop sign and took a right turn heading for the restaurant, which sat just a few hundred yards away. There were cars in the parking lot – always a good sign. As he pulled into the lot, his hope of finding a meal dissipated. Yellow police tape stretched from one side of the building to the other. Further inspection showed the establishment had suffered a recent fire. That there weren't any spirits lingering out front was a good sign. Several men stood behind the yellow tape near the front entrance. Two had clipboards in their hands and looked up as he drove past. Jerry waved and kept on going – driving to the end of the lot, where he stopped to check for an alternative route. The ramp closure must have been recent, as it still wasn't registering on his navigator. Jerry thumbed through the settings and changed his preference to avoid the interstate. It worked as the navigator now instructed him to go in the opposite direction of the ramp.

As soon as he started down the two-lane road, his feeling of unease intensified. He was about to say as much when Gunter suddenly appeared in the front seat wearing the K-9 police vest he'd worn when on duty with the Pennsylvania State Police.

Something's wrong.

Jerry pressed on the gas pedal and followed the pull that now drew him forward as if being reeled in from a fishing pole. Jerry leaned forward in his seat as if doing so would get him wherever he was going faster. He started into a blind curve, and Gunter barked a frantic warning. Jerry eased off the gas, a good thing because a brown Econoline van was stopped in the center of the road. Two legs stuck out underneath the back of the van, toes face up. In the grass to the right, a dark-haired woman in brightly colored overall capris stood holding an infant in one arm, and waved to get his attention with the other. Jerry veered to the left, sliding to a screeching halt just inches away from the legs, which never moved.

Jerry turned on his emergency flashers and jumped from the SUV. His first thought was that the woman had hit someone, dragging the body under her vehicle until coming to a stop. This thought passed as he grew closer to the van and heard a male voice singing out of tune from beneath. Jerry looked up and saw the woman picking her way through the grass toward him. The woman didn't seem to be in a hurry to reach him, so Jerry turned his attention back to the feet. Gunter beat him to the man, sniffed the shoes, then walked a few feet and peed an invisible stream on the van's right rear tire.

Jerry, being more of the curious sort, kicked the man's boot with his own. The boot kicked forward, and a few seconds later, the body scrambled out from under the van. He smiled at Jerry and removed an earbud from his ear. Covered in grease to his elbows, he looked at Jerry's Durango, then back toward the woman holding the baby, who was just approaching the back of the van. "See, Cathy, I told you someone would come along eventually."

Jerry didn't have time for pleasantries. "What's wrong with the van?"

"Not really sure. I'm not a mechanic."

Cathy laughed. "He's right about that. We've been stuck out here in the heat for over an hour. He won't even let me get in the van to change the baby."

"Smart man. I didn't see you until I was halfway into the curve." Jerry wanted to tell them the only reason he didn't slam into them was that Gunter had warned him in time to stop. The tingling sensation had lessened, but it was still crawling up his neck, letting him know that while he'd found what he was looking for, the danger had not passed. Jerry knew his Durango would take the brunt if someone were to run into them, not that it mattered – if they were hit by someone doing the speed limit, it would push his Durango into the van, possibly killing them all. Jerry looked over his shoulder. "I'm going to move my ride to the lip of the curb to help slow people down."

The woman switched the baby to the opposite hip and bounced it up and down. "I don't know why you're bothering. You're the first person to come through since we broke down."

"Leave the man alone, Cathy. He's trying to help."

The woman ignored him. "You know anything about vans, mister?"

Jerry shook his head. "No, ma'am."

She looked at her husband. "That makes two of you."

The man raised an eyebrow. "She's not usually this cranky. She's prego."

Jerry glanced at the woman and, for the first time, noticed the bulge. That it was over ninety degrees out and the child in her arms didn't look old enough to walk probably didn't help her mood. "Let me reposition my ride, and I'll call for a tow truck."

The man frowned. Cathy looked at the baby and shook her head. "No. We can't afford one of those. It might take a bit, but Bobby will get it fixed. He always does."

Jerry rubbed at the back of his neck. "Do you have a chain? I can at least pull you off the road."

Bobby bobbed his head. "It's in the back."

"Get it."

Gunter growled and turned toward the bend in the curb. Jerry's heart sank. "Move back. Someone is coming!"

Cathy hesitated. "I don't hear anything."

Before Jerry could respond, Gunter raced down

the street in the direction they'd just come from. Jerry ran after him and saw a semi-truck heading straight for them. He yelled for Bobby to get his wife out of the way and waved his hands to get the driver's attention. The man didn't react. *Stop looking at your phone.*

Gunter stood his ground, standing between Jerry and the truck. The dog's head was up, his tail erect, as he barked to get the driver's attention. Jerry yelled for Gunter to move. The driver looked up, took in the scene, and yanked the steering wheel to the right. The trailer's wheels locked, sending black smoke billowing through the air. The semi traveled through the muddy cornfield for some time, leaving a path the width of his truck in its wake. A pickup truck following the tractor-trailer slid to a stop sideways across the road.

Jerry looked for Gunter, but the dog was nowhere in sight. Jerry looked over the scene and pressed his palms together, bringing his fingertips to his lips. *Thank you for letting me be here. Please let Gunter be okay.* Recovering, Jerry ran to the pickup to check on the driver. "You okay?"

"I am. I'm not sure how he's going to get that truck out of there. It's been raining for a week. That field is drenched."

Serves him right. "You got a phone?"

"Don't everyone?"

Perhaps. But it doesn't mean they have the sense

to use it. Jerry kept the thought to himself. "Move your truck to the other side of the curb and turn on your flashers."

"I got some flares too."

"Good man. Use them."

Jerry ran into the field. Sure enough, five steps in, he sank to his ankles. He slowed his pace, reaching the truck just as the driver got out of the cab. Jerry struggled to keep his voice calm. "Are you alright?"

"Yes, no thanks to you. What the heck were you and that dog doing in the center of the road?"

Jerry narrowed his eyes. "What dog?"

"The shepherd. Don't tell me you didn't see him?"

"All I saw was you looking at your freaking phone."

"I was trying to find a way back onto the interstate. The blasted on-ramp is closed. Now it's going to cost me a small fortune to get my truck drug out of this field."

"You're lucky that's all you're going to have to pay for."

"What's that supposed to mean?"

"Just around that bend is a van stalled in the middle of the road. Standing in the grass next to it is a young pregnant woman with a baby on her hip. Her husband was under the van trying to fix it when I came upon them a few moments ago. If you hadn't looked up when you did, you would have probably killed the whole family." Jerry didn't bother to point out the fact that he was so preoccupied with his cell phone that he hadn't even realized he was heading into a curve. Nor that he was going so fast, he probably wouldn't have been able to maintain control of his truck. If not for fate placing Jerry and Gunter at the scene, the whole situation could have ended worse than anyone could imagine. On the plus side, the imminent doom Jerry had felt was now gone or would be once he was reunited with his dog.

Chapter Two

Jerry used Bobby's chain to tow the van to the side of the road, then sat in his Durango waiting for the tow truck to haul the van to the shop. The trucker contacted a semi wrecker service an hour away and climbed in the back of his sleeper, refusing to speak to anyone at the scene. Bobby crawled back under the van, declaring he'd fix the thing before paying for repairs. Jerry offered to let Cathy and the baby sit in the Durango's air, but she'd refused, saying she wanted to get the baby down for a short nap while they waited. Once the van was safely off the road, the man driving the pickup continued on his way. Even though Jerry felt the danger was over, he decided to wait behind the van so that anyone coming around the curve would see his emergency flashers.

In for a penny, in for a pound. Jerry smiled. It was a saying his granny had used often over the years. Jerry looked in the rearview mirror, half expecting the woman to be sitting there. He heaved a heavy sigh when neither she nor Gunter showed themselves. *Easy, McNeal, don't go getting yourself all worked up. The dog will return. He always does.* Jerry closed his eyes and pressed his head into the back of the seat.

***

Jerry stood in the shower letting the water run over the top of his head. He picked up the washcloth and ran it across his face; once, twice, three times. Jerry opened his eyes, realized he'd fallen asleep, and struggled to focus on his surroundings. Just as his brain caught up with the fact he was still in the Durango waiting for the wrecker to arrive, Gunter's tongue snaked across his cheek. Jerry wrestled with the decision to either push the K-9 away or embrace the ghostly spirit. His heart won out, and he wrapped an arm around the dog while simultaneously wiping the slobber from his cheek.

Jerry laughed. "How is it you can lift your leg without making a stream, and yet my face is so wet, I was dreaming I was in the shower?"

Gunter lifted his lips and smiled a K-9 smile.

Jerry let go of the animal and gave him a firm pat. "Glad to have you back, dog."

Gunter answered with a single woof and wag of the tail. There was a rumbling in the distance, and the dog whipped his head around. Jerry looked in the rearview mirror to see a midsize tow truck rounding the bend. It slowed, then drove past him, maneuvering in front of the Econoline. Jerry got out of the SUV just as Bobby slid from under the van.

Still covered in grease, Bobby yawned and stretched his arms, giving Jerry the distinct impression the man had been sleeping.

A tall, lanky fellow, wearing a blue work shirt and jeans, jumped down from the cab of the tow truck. The embroidered name patch on the front of his shirt sported the name Dale.

Dale looked between Jerry and Bobby, his attention settling on the latter. "What seems to be the trouble with her?"

"Danged if I know. The wife heard a noise in the back just before it died."

Dale frowned. "What kind of noise?"

"Didn't hear it myself." Bobby tilted his head to show an earbud protruding from his left ear canal. "The baby was crying, so I had the music turned up to drown out the noise."

Jerry raised an eyebrow, but Dale beat him to the punch. "You do know it's illegal to drive with those things in, right?"

Bobby shrugged. "Everyone does it."

Jerry hauled off and punched Bobby right in the mouth. Bobby laughed at something Dale said, and Jerry realized he'd not actually hit the man. Jerry shook off the vision and ran a hand over his head to calm himself. He crooked a finger toward Bobby. "Come with me."

Bobby hesitated then followed. Jerry led him down the road and pointed at the semi, which still sat in the heavily damaged cornfield. "Do you know why that man's in the field?"

"Because he's a bad driver?"

Partly. "Because he was texting and driving. The driver was distracted. He could've killed you, your wife, and both your kids."

"We only have one." Bobby's eyes lit up, and he smiled. "Oh, you were counting the one in the oven. Good one."

"Driving distracted is a stupid thing to do. It doesn't matter if the distraction is texting on the phone or wearing earbuds."

Bobby rocked back on his heels and grinned. "Nah, earbuds don't count. I could still see."

Jerry nodded toward the van. "Did you hear the noise the van made in time to get it out of the road and see your family safe?"

The smile vanished. "No. I guess I see what you mean. I didn't mean no harm. I just couldn't handle all the crying. You don't know what it's like."

Jerry thought back to his trip from Pennsylvania to Kentucky, listening to Cat squalling his indignation the entire way. At one point, he'd turned up the radio in an attempt to drown out the cat's meows. He sighed. "Listen, Bobby, I know you didn't mean to put your family in harm's way, but whether you meant to or not, it happened. Let this be a lesson you learn from. Cathy is pregnant, and she needs your help."

Bobby held up his hands. “I don’t do diapers.”

Jerry suddenly regretted not actually clocking the man. He flexed his fingers to keep from doing so. “How about we start with the basics? If either of the babies are crying so much that you have difficulty driving, pull over for a bit. And not on the side of the road. Find a rest stop or parking lot. Then offer to take the other kid for a walk while Cathy quiets the one who is upset. Can you do that?”

Bobby looked toward the van and nodded his head. “I guess so.”

Jerry smiled. “Good. You know what they say: happy wife, happy life.”

Bobby’s eyes grew wide. “That’s another good one. Cathy does seem to yell less when she’s happy.”

Imagine that. Jerry worked to keep his sarcasm in check. “Speaking of Cathy and the baby, how about you go and get them out of the van.”

Bobby frowned. “Why?”

Jerry glanced at Gunter, who was standing right next to the guy, half expecting the dog to roll his eyes. When the dog didn’t respond, Jerry turned his attention back to Bobby. “Because people are not allowed to ride in a vehicle while it’s being towed.”

Bobby gulped, and his Adam’s apple bobbed. “You mean we’re going to have to walk?”

Jerry clamped him on the shoulder, turning him toward the van. “If the driver doesn’t let you ride with him, I'll give you a lift to the next town."

Jerry followed Bobby back to the van and craned his neck to peek inside. The van had been converted into a camper with a bed lengthwise across the back. Cathy was lying on the bed with the baby, who was awake and cooing at the ceiling. The sun streamed through the window, casting a red hue over Cathy's brown locks. Instantly, the inside of the van was white and devoid of everything but the bed. A woman with brilliant red hair lay on the mattress and stared out at him with vacant eyes. The woman's spirit rose from her body, and she reached a hand to him. "Help us, Jerry. You're the only one."

Jerry's mouth watered, his stomach flipping with a wave of nausea that nearly sent him to his knees. Gunter whined as Jerry backed from the van, struggling to regain his composure.

"You alright there, Buddy?"

Jerry looked up to see the tow truck driver staring at him with knitted brows. He waved the guy off, resting his palm on the side of the hot metal to steady himself. "I'm good. I think the woman changed a dirty diaper in there." It was a lie but better than telling the man of the vision he'd just had.

Dale laughed. "Easy to tell you don't have kids. I have four myself – can't imagine my life without them."

Jerry checked to see if Bobby was standing near.

He wasn't. "I'll have Cathy and the baby ride with me. You take Bobby. Perhaps you can share some parenting wisdom with that dude on your way back to the shop. He seems to think raising a kid is his wife's job."

Dale grinned. "I do love me a captive audience."

***

Jerry stood in the garage bay, waiting for the mechanic to give an estimate for the repair. The shop was a small family-run business. Dale had phoned his brother Carl on the way in and asked him to come have a look at the van as a favor to Jerry, who'd offered to pay the bill for the couple, who didn't have the funds to pay for the repair themselves. Carl was a shorter, heavier version of Dale, but the resemblance was enough to see they were brothers. Carl sauntered over to Jerry, wiping his hands on a rag. "Dale said you're willing to pay the damages."

Jerry nodded. "That's right."

"You kin?"

"No." *Not that it's any of your business.*

"One of those good Samaritans then."

Jerry wasn't in the mood to discuss his reasons for paying the bill. "What's wrong with it, and how much?"

"Take it easy. I'm getting to it. It's the crankshaft position sensor. Easy enough to replace, but it won't be until morning. The auto store is closed for the night. You should get out of here for just under three hundred, providing they have the part in stock."

Three hundred plus a night in the motel since they won't be able to sleep in the van. Jerry cocked his head toward the van. "The wife said she heard a clicking noise before the van stopped."

"That's what my brother said. I went over it. Near as I can tell, what the woman heard was a rock in the tire."

Jerry looked at the van once more. "What about the grease the guy had all over him?"

Carl snickered. "My guess is the guy was simply touching things just to let the woman think he knew what he was doing."

"You sure?"

"Listen, Buddy, if you want to pay more, I'll be happy to make something up. But the sensor is all I found wrong with the thing."

Jerry shook his head. "I plan on heading out soon. I just wanted to make sure they'll be able to get on their way tomorrow."

"I expect the auto store to have the part. If not, I'll see they have a place to sleep until I get it fixed." Carl looked directly at Gunter, yet there was no evidence the man saw anything other than the garage floor. "You ain't the only good Samaritan around, you know."

Jerry smiled. "Glad to see there are still good people in the world."

Carl winked. "Right back at ya."

"Can I pay now? I want to get on my way."

The man furrowed his brow, once again showing the resemblance to his brother. "The card machine is offline for the night. I guess I can trust you for an out-of-state check."

Jerry reached for his wallet. "I was thinking of paying cash."

The furrowed brow was replaced with a wide grin. "Cash is good."

Jerry doled out three one-hundred-dollar bills, handing them to the man. He pulled out another fifty, offering it as well. "Thank you for coming in after hours."

Carl waved him off. "I didn't do anything I wouldn't have done for anyone else."

"Are you sure?"

Carl nodded. "Pop made a good name doing business this way. He always said being flexible is just good business."

Jerry tucked the bill back inside his wallet. "Your pop sounds like a good man."

"The best. He took Dale and me in when we were kids. We'd both had a rough go of it going from one foster home to the other. We'd made a pack to stay together after our ma died – our pa was a drunk and didn't have any time for us, so we got put in the system. Every time someone would try to split us up, we'd do something to get sent back. I got sent to Pop and Martha's first. They were nice enough, but Dale and I'd made that pact. So I did everything I could to get sent back. Then one day, Pop sat me down and asked why I kept acting up. He pressed me until I told him I wanted to go back to where my brother was. He looked at me like I had two heads and said, 'Wouldn't it be better to bring your brother here?' I don't think either of us ever got into trouble after that – nothing major anyway. We've always done our best to follow in his footsteps and do everything we could to make him proud of us. We take pride in running the place the way he always did. I hope he knows what an impact he had on us."

Jerry looked at the spirit of the older gentleman who'd been lingering in the corner ever since he'd arrived. The spirit winked and positioned his hand into a thumbs-up motion. Jerry mimicked the man's action. "I'm sure he knows how you feel."

Carl's jaw dropped open. "Wow. That's crazy weird. Pops used to do the same thing."

Jerry slid another glance to the spirit, stealthily motioned Gunter to his side, and left without comment.

Chapter Three

While Jerry was glad he'd been there to help, he couldn't help thinking he'd wasted valuable time. With everything under control, he was eager to be on his way to Salem. Jerry opened the door to the Durango, stepping aside as Gunter jumped in and moved to the passenger seat. The dog poked his head out the window while Jerry scrolled through the navigator and changed the settings back to the fastest route before leaving the parking lot. As he drove, he replayed the happenings of the day and the random series of events that saved the lives of Bobby, Cathy, and their baby.

"Don't forget the driver of the semi. If you hadn't been there, things could have been worse for the man."

Jerry looked in the mirror to see his grandmother smiling back at him. An instant later, the woman traded places with Gunter. Not wishing to be ignored, Gunter craned his head through the opening between the seats, smothering the woman's spirit with K-9 kisses.

Jerry nodded toward the dog. "I guess I'm not the

only one happy to see you."

Granny laughed and motioned for Gunter to get back. "He sees me plenty enough. Who do you think looks after him on the other side?"

Jerry slid a glance to the passenger seat. "Did the truck hit him? It looked like it did, then when he showed up, he didn't have a scratch on him."

"The dog's body has taken its licks since attaching himself to you. But his spirit is intact."

"I know I'm not supposed to ask, but I don't understand how any of this works." Jerry ran a hand over his head and continued before she could stop him. "The dog is dead. His body is buried in a grave in Pennsylvania. So how can his body be taking licks, and how many licks can he take before he can't come around anymore?"

His grandmother sighed a heavy sigh. "You worry too much, Jerry."

Jerry couldn't argue. He'd been worrying about things that were out of his control for as long as he could recall. "I think in this case I have reason to worry. Since he's been with me, he's been shot, stabbed, and now hit by a truck." Jerry wasn't totally sure about the truck, but the dog had disappeared for a while after the incident.

Granny pulled her fingers across her lips as if zipping them shut.

Jerry drummed his fingers on the steering wheel. "At least tell me how many times he's allowed to come back."

"Why? So you can protect him?"

Yes. "Maybe."

"No."

"No, what?"

"No, you don't get to have all the answers. And you are not in the Marines anymore."

"What does the Marines have to do with this?"

"It is not your mission to fix everything. You need to stop trying to protect the dog and let Gunter do his job."

"Which is?"

"Whatever it needs to be."

"That's pretty broad."

She shrugged. "It is what it is."

"So you're saying he's my guardian angel."

"I don't recall using those words."

"You're even more confusing than when you were alive."

"Thank you." Granny laced her fingers and rested them on her stomach, looking quite pleased with herself.

Jerry opened his mouth to remind his grandmother she'd forgotten to put on her seatbelt, then silently chided himself at the absurdity. "It wasn't a compliment."

She turned toward him and grinned. "I know."

The navigator signaled him to turn to get on the highway. Jerry reduced his speed and turned on his blinker.

Granny placed a hand on his arm. “Go straight.”

Jerry followed her instructions without hesitation. “Where am I going?”

“Don’t you remember?”

Jerry chuckled. “Well, I was going to Salem before you made me miss my turn.”

“Just because you know where you’re going doesn’t mean you need to be in a hurry to get there. Do you realize you went to Niagara Falls without seeing more than a glimpse of them? What’s the point of traveling the world if you’re not going to take a moment to see where you are going?” Granny leaned her head against the seat.

“Are you going to sleep?”

“We don’t need sleep.”

“I’ve seen Gunter sleep.”

“You’ve seen the dog mimic his earthly counterparts.”

In more ways than one. “He’s good at being a dog.”

“That’s because he is a dog.”

“You’re giving me a headache.”

Granny disappeared.

Jerry looked in the mirror at Gunter. “Was it something I said?”

Gunter groaned.

“This will help.” Jerry looked to see Granny sitting next to him, holding two paper cups. She offered him one.

"What's this?"

"Chamomile tea. It's good for headaches."

"I don't have a headache. I said you were giving me one."

"I went to the trouble to make it, so you might as well drink it."

"You made it?" Jerry sniffed the cup and took a drink, finding it surprisingly good.

"Of course, I made it. I'm a spirit, not a magician."

Jerry sat the cup in the center holder. He ran his hand over his head and pulled to the side of the road.

"What are you doing?"

"Changing the navigator." He winked and grinned a wide grin. "Some of us are not all-knowing."

"You know more than you think you do."

"Meaning?"

"In all your years when you set your mind to something, has your inner radar ever failed you?"

Jerry started to think about her question.

"This isn't a test. I'm telling you to let your gift guide you."

"I can't."

She opened her eyes and peered at him. "And why not?"

"Because things get in the way. I have a purpose now. You know that. You're the one that helped me realize it."

"And you'll continue to help them. I know you now have a purpose, but that doesn't mean doing that one thing to the detriment of others who could benefit from what you have to offer. If we hadn't gotten you off that highway, you wouldn't have been there to save that family."

"That trucker would have swerved before he got to them," Jerry countered.

"And the pickup truck driver would have been so busy avoiding the semi, he would have plowed right into them."

"You said you got me off the highway?"

"I had a bit of help, but yes."

"If you know what's going to happen, why not just tell me so I can go wherever it is I'm supposed to be and wait."

Granny reached a hand and patted his arm. "Don't be in such a hurry to get where you are going."

"Why? Is something going to happen?"

"I just want you to enjoy this life you've been given. You have a gift. Slow down and take time to enjoy it, and when the opportunity arises, use it to help others."

The dashboard lit up, announcing Savannah's call. Jerry started to say something to Granny, but the seat where she'd been sitting was now empty. Jerry sighed and pressed his finger to the screen to answer the call. “Hello?”

“Hey, stranger. Life keeping you busy?”

Jerry laughed. “Life, death; sometimes it all blends together.”

“Max told me about Ashley.”

“There was another one after that.”

“Really?”

“Yes, a woman by the name of Rita.”

“Are they connected?”

“I’d stake my life on it.”

“If you need any help, let me know.”

“Will do. How’s Max? I’m glad she reached out to you.”

“She’s a great kid. I’m not sure how much help I’ll be, but I’ll try.”

Jerry frowned at the dash. “Is there a problem?”

Laughter drifted through the speakers. “Only that she’s better than me. If you tell her that, I’ll deny it. Seriously, that girl has some mondo talent. She just doesn’t know it yet. She told me what you did.”

“What would that be?”

“Giving her and her mom the reward money. You are one of the good guys.”

Jerry shrugged off the compliment. “Of course I gave it to them. Max earned it. If not for her, I wouldn’t have even gone to Michigan.”

“Just take the compliment, Jerry. It won’t kill you to admit you’re a good guy.” Savannah continued without waiting for him to respond. “I think her mom might have a little psychic ability too. Just a hunch, but I'll let you know if it proves to be so."

"I've often wondered about that."

"About Max's mom?"

"No, people in general. Mom said she didn't have it, but there were times when she seemed to know things."

"It can skip a generation. Maybe your mom had something, but not enough to be considered clairvoyant."

"You're probably right about it skipping. If Mom had the gift, Granny would have known."

"How is she?"

"Mom?"

"Her too, but I was talking about Granny. She's there with you, isn't she?"

Jerry glanced at the passenger seat. "Not anymore, but she was when you called."

"Yep, I'm that good." Savannah laughed. "Granny's visit, was it a social call or more?"

"I haven't figured it out yet."

"Meaning?"

"I'm on my way to Salem."

"Where the witch trials were? Cool! I bet there are some wicked winds there."

"Wicked winds?"

"Yeah, you know, ghosts, spirits, and energy in the air."

Jerry eyed the dashboard. "And what precisely is the difference between ghosts and spirits?"

"I don't know."

"Nothing. That's what. And just to be clear, Granny said they prefer 'spirits' instead of 'ghosts'."

"Is Gunter with you?"

"He's in the back."

"Can he hear me?"

"Why don't you ask him?"

"Gunter?"

To Jerry's surprise, the dog appeared in the passenger seat. He tilted his head, looking at the dash. "Would you believe me if I told you he's listening?"

Savannah's voice turned serious. "After all we've been through, I'd probably believe just about anything you told me."

"Ditto. He's listening. Go ahead with your question."

"Gunter, are you a spirit?"

Gunter bared his teeth and growled a grumbling growl.

"He didn't seem to like the question."

"So I noticed."

"Gunter? Are you a ghost?"

Gunter lifted his head, barking his enthusiasm.

"See, there is a difference."

Jerry gave Gunter a pat to settle him. "You just might be right."

"Of course I am. Hey, I told Max I was going to call you, and she wanted me to pass along the number 207."

"What's that?"

"We were hoping you'd know. Max blurted it out the moment I mentioned your name."

"Nothing comes to mind."

"It seemed pretty important, but she said it was too early. Just keep your eye out. She also said to tell Gunter hello."

Gunter barked.

Jerry shook his head. "Keep this up, and the dog's going to want his own cell phone."

"You changed the subject."

"What?"

"I asked why Granny showed up, and you changed the subject."

"No, I was telling you about the…never mind." Arguing with Savannah never ended in his favor. "I took the wrong exit and ended up maybe saving some lives."

"What do you mean 'maybe'? Did you or didn't you?"

"Probably, but you can't prove a negative."

"What's that supposed to mean?"

"I was there, and they didn't die. But that doesn't mean they would have died if I wasn't there."

"Same old Jerry. Still running from your gift."

Jerry thought about hanging up on her but knew

she'd keep calling back until he finally answered. The worst part was she was right. "Fine, yes, someone – possibly all – would have died if I wasn't there."

Gunter barked, then bared his teeth in a menacing growl.

"He's mad you're taking all the credit."

Jerry blinked at the dash. "It doesn't take a clairvoyant to figure that out."

"Sorry, just trying to help."

"Anyway, when all was said and done, and I was trying to get back on the highway, Granny showed up and told me I needed to slow down."

"Were you speeding?"

"Not in the physical sense. Life in general."

"She has a point. It's not like you have a real job."

"Ouch."

"I didn't mean it like that, and you know it. What I meant is you're not punching the clock, so why break your neck to get where you're going."

"Because there's a serial killer on the loose! That's why." Jerry realized he'd yelled and sighed. "Sorry for yelling. It's just that there is a guy out there killing women, and I seem to be the only one who can find him."

"That's a pretty heavy weight to carry, but your granny's right. Three innocent people could have died today if you had stayed on your path."

"Four…no…five, if you want to get technical. The woman was pregnant."

"And me and Alex, and God knows how many other people you've saved, just by being there at the right time."

Gunter pawed at the dash and growled a low growl.

"Sorry. You too, Gunter."

Gunter wagged his tail and yipped at the screen.

"I think you're forgiven."

"See, even ghosts can't stay mad at me. Listen, I know you want to catch the guy, and my gut tells me you will. But listen to your granny. She seems to know what she's talking about."

Jerry laughed.

"What's so funny?"

"We are hundreds of miles apart, talking through my vehicle's speakers about taking the advice of a woman who has been dead for years. Seltzer always tells me I lead some life. I'm starting to believe him."

"Maybe I should give him a call. It sounds like you'd listen to him."

"Nah, he's a cop. He'd tell me to quit messing around and solve the case."

"You think so?"

Jerry laughed once more. "I'm sure of it. Only there'd be a few swear words involved."

"That's what's different. I knew there was

something but couldn't quite put my finger on it."

"Care to fill me in?"

"You haven't said a single swear word this whole conversation."

"Just trying to clean up my act is all."

"Why?"

"When I was talking to Max, I let a few slip. She said it was alright, that she'd heard them in school. But it didn't feel right. Hey, I'm getting into a bad area, so I'm going to let you go." Jerry disconnected the call before she caught him in the lie. The moment the call ended, Gunter yawned. "What?"

Gunter yawned a second time.

"If it's all the same to you, I'd like you to stop judging me."

Gunter turned away from him.

"Okay, so I told a white lie. If I'd stayed on the phone, she would have caught me in another. The truth of the matter is I'm still holding on to hope that I'll hear from Holly. If I do, I want to make sure I don't slip up and say something inappropriate in front of her kid." Jerry felt an instant relief at having finally told someone. It didn't matter that the someone was a dog who would never understand what he was talking about.

Gunter turned in his seat and sat facing Jerry. After a moment, he relaxed and lowered to where his head was resting on the console watching him with sorrowful golden brown eyes. Jerry recalled the canine's recent encounter with Lady, the jet-black German shepherd they'd camped next to in Michigan. Jerry reached over and scratched the dog behind the ear. "I guess we're both members of the lonely hearts club, huh, Buddy."

Gunter lifted his head and gave a low, soulful howl. Jerry gripped the wheel, opened his mouth, and joined him.

Chapter Four

It was late when Jerry arrived in Salem. While the streets were not empty, they were devoid of heavy traffic. He drove through town trying to get a lead on Rosie Freeman, sighing when, after a second pass, his psychic radar failed to home in on the woman.

Jerry glanced at Gunter, and the dog's ears perked up. "I'm not getting anything, are you?"

Jerry took Gunter's lack of response as a no. "What say we call it a day and start new in the morning?"

Gunter replied with a single sharp bark of approval.

Jerry circled back around to where he'd seen a few hotels. Not getting a hit on any building in particular, he chose one with open parking spaces, hoping he'd have a chance at getting a room without a reservation. Jerry backed into a parking spot and turned to look at Gunter. "This looks as good as any. What do you say?"

Gunter groaned.

"What?"

The dog looked toward the hotel sign and barked a questioning bark.

Jerry raised an eyebrow. Surely the dog hadn't caught on to the fact he'd also chosen it because of the name. Hollydaze Inn – it reminded him of Holly.

He glanced at the dog, who lifted his lips in a ghostly K-9 smile. Jerry laughed a hearty laugh. "You sure are something, dog."

Jerry reached for his cell phone and saw he had a message from Seltzer. He clicked on the message, which simply read *Just checking in. Are you still in Niagara Falls?* Jerry rolled his neck. For someone who wasn't supposed to have anything tying him down, he sure seemed to have a lot of people keeping tabs on him. He pressed reply. "No, Dad. I'm partying in Salem."

Jerry hit send. He'd barely pocketed the phone before the dash lit up, alerting him to Seltzer's call. He thought about not answering, but the man already knew he was awake. "Yes?"

"What in blue blazes are you doing in Massachusetts?" Though the man's voice was riddled with the worried tone of a harried father, they were not kin. Not by blood anyway. Seltzer had looked out for him so often over the years that he could easily qualify for an honorary title.

Jerry instantly regretted sending the snide reply. "I'm here looking for Rosie Freeman."

"Should I know that name?"

"She was on the list you sent."

"So she's dead?"

"I haven't found her yet, so I can't say for sure."

"What do your spidey senses tell you?"

"Nothing."

"Is that normal?"

Jerry laughed. "Is anything with me normal?"

Seltzer ignored the comment. "So what happened in New York?"

"I found the girl and had a visit from Fred and Barney." Jerry had debated telling his former boss about the most recent visit from the two but thought it time to bring him into the loop.

"Fabel's goons?"

"I thought so at first, but too much cloak and dagger."

"How so?"

"They weren't very forthcoming with their identity but alluded to the fact they could lock me away."

"Why am I just now hearing of this?"

"Because I didn't want to get you more involved."

"I'm a cop. It's my job to be involved."

"This isn't cop business. Not Pennsylvania cop anyway."

"What did they want?"

"The same thing everyone else wants – to know how I come to figure out where the bodies are buried when no one else can." Jerry grew quiet for a moment. "You should know they pulled a Fabel."

"How's that?"

"Used you as leverage to get me to talk."

"Did it work?"

"You're not in jail, and my spidey senses tell me I'm not talking to a ghost."

This time, it was Seltzer who was quiet. Jerry heard a sigh. "So, how did you leave it with those two?"

"I told them where to find Rita's body and told them I was heading to Massachusetts."

"And they were alright with you leaving."

"I got the impression they would have no trouble finding me."

Another sigh. "Unless Fabel's men find you first."

"Guess I won't have trouble getting a dinner date if I need one."

Gunter growled a deep warning and Jerry looked to see a black sedan creeping through the parking lot. "Easy boy."

"What's wrong with the dog?"

"I think one of my dates just arrived to tuck me into bed."

"I'm catching a plane."

"No!"

"And why not?"

"You'd only get in the way. I can't watch my

back and yours too." The sedan drove past and then left the parking lot without stopping.

"At least tell me which team your visitors are playing for."

"Can't. The windows were too tinted to see. That they didn't stop tells me it was probably team Flintstone."

"Do they know what room you are in?"

"No."

"How can you be sure?"

"Because I haven't checked in yet."

"Text me your hotel and room information as soon as you get settled."

Jerry chuckled.

"I'm glad you find this amusing."

Jerry shook his head. "I don't. It's just been a long time since I had to tell anyone where I was going."

"While we're at it, go to bed, and don't let me hear of you roaming the streets tonight." The concern came from a good place and reminded him of simpler times when his real father had given him similar warnings. Only his father had done so to instill fear over a child. A chilling warning of the proverbial boogie man was a scare tactic parents had often used to keep children from going astray. The thing was, Jerry had long since learned that the boogie man was the least of his worries. The dead didn't hurt you. Not as a rule anyway.

Jerry rolled his neck. "The only thing I want to do tonight is get some shuteye."

"Gunter?" Seltzer's voice sang out through the speakers.

Gunter looked at the dash and cocked his head to the side, his long, pointed ears brushing the back of the seat.

"He's listening."

"YOU WATCH JERRY'S BACK, TROOPER. THAT'S AN ORDER!"

Gunter disappeared and reappeared an instant later wearing his police harness. He fixated on Jerry, barking his understanding.

"Did he hear me?"

"I think the whole block heard you."

This time when Seltzer spoke, his voice was considerably lower. "Sorry. I got carried away. I guess it is a good thing June isn't home."

"Still in North Carolina?"

"For three more days."

"How are you holding up?"

"I'm down to my last pair of skivvies."

Jerry laughed. "I wasn't talking about your underwear."

"I know. As for June, she and her sister are still under surveillance by my guy."

"Good. As for your underwear, watch a YouTube video and learn how to do laundry."

"I can tell you've never been married."

"Why's that?"

"If my wife comes home and everything is in place, it will look like I don't need her."

"Won't she be upset if she has to clean up your mess?"

"Sure. She'll fuss and carry on, but deep down, she'll know I can't make it without her."

Jerry wasn't so sure. "And you think she'll be happier if she comes home to a mess than a clean house?"

"Son, it's just as well you're not married. You've got a lot to learn about women."

Jerry looked at the sign that displayed the name of the hotel and sighed.

"You sound tired. Are your friends gone?"

Jerry scanned the parking lot. "Seem to be."

"Okay. If you see them again, snap a photo and send it to me. If you go missing, I want to know where to start looking."

Crap. McNeal, you're falling down on the job. Why didn't you think of that? Jerry was about to say as much when he remembered the camera in the bar. "You got any friends in New York?"

"A few, why?"

"See if you can get someone to check the cameras in the Willow Tree Bar from two nights ago. I was sitting in the corner booth when Fred and Barney joined me. Should be somewhere between nine and ten."

"I'll see what I can find out. Take care of yourself, McNeal."

"Will do, Sarge."

Jerry ended the call and turned off the ignition. He exited the Durango, and Gunter hung back. "What's up with you, dog?"

Gunter yawned.

Jerry scanned the area but didn't see anything amiss. Closing the door, he circled the SUV to grab his bags. It was then he saw he'd parked in front of a light pole. Normally, doing so wouldn't bother him, but this time, the hairs on the back of his neck stood on end. Jerry returned to the driver's seat and moved the Durango to a new spot several spaces over. Turning off the ignition, he opened the door. This time, Gunter was happy to follow.

Hollydaze Inn looked the same as most in the popular chain, this one standing four stories. Jerry threw his seabag over his left shoulder and carried both his gun bag and mesh dirty clothes bag in the same hand, leaving his right hand free in case it was needed. Gunter wore his police vest and stayed glued to his side as they walked across the parking lot.

Even though Jerry didn't feel uneasy, he breathed a sigh of relief when they entered the building. The front desk area was empty when he approached.

"I'll be right with you," a man's voice called

from behind an open wall.

Jerry placed his bags on the floor beside him and waited.

A blonde-haired man who looked to be in his early twenties, wearing a white button-up shirt with sleeves rolled to the elbow, sauntered around the opening. The copper-colored nametag on the front of his shirt showed his name to be Kenny Nunes. Kenny eyed Jerry as he screwed the top on a bottle of Mountain Dew. Setting the bottle on the counter, he smiled. "Good evening, sir. Do you have a reservation?"

Jerry shook his head. "No. I hope that won't be a problem."

"Your name?"

"Jerry McNeal."

The man's cheeks turned pink as he studied the monitor. "I have one room left. A king suite."

Jerry pulled his wallet from his pocket and slid his credit card across the counter.

Kenny keyed in the numbers and returned the card along with an envelope with a key card. Jerry opened the envelope and read the room number. Two-zero-seven. The same number Max had keyed on.

Jerry started to return his wallet to his pocket, then hesitated. He pulled out a hundred and slid the bill across the counter. Kenny reached for the bill, and Jerry held it in place with the tips of his fingers.

Kenny's eyes widened.

Jerry met the man's gaze. "Anyone comes looking for me, I ain't here. That goes for phone calls too. You are to tell no one what room I'm in."

Kenny swallowed and bobbed his head up and down.

Jerry smiled and released the bill. Picking up his bags, he headed to the elevator with Gunter at his side. As the door slid closed, Jerry looked to Gunter. "Something about that guy rubs me the wrong way. He don't hold up his part of the bargain, he's all yours."

Gunter bared his teeth, growled a menacing growl, and wagged his tail.

Chapter Five

The suite was more than adequate for a single man, even one traveling with a ninety-pound ghost dog. The bed looked enticing, even though it held enough pillows to satisfy an entire family. Further surveying the room, he noted a couch, easy chair, desk with computer chair, and a long counter with a sink and microwave. The bathroom was oversized, with everything a hotel bathroom should have. Just to the left of the couch was a door to the adjoining room. If not for being told he'd claimed the last room, Jerry would have asked to change rooms – especially since Max had keyed on the room number. Jerry sat his seabag on the folding platform normally reserved for suitcases and shoved his gun bag in the closet. He walked to the other side of the room and tested the adjoining door to confirm it was locked.

Jerry checked the alarm clock to ensure it was turned off and eyed the bed, wishing nothing more than to flop on top and sleep until housekeeping woke him while vacuuming the outside hallway. As it was, he had a ditty bag full of laundry that wasn't going to wash itself, and he knew from experience the best time to do laundry was late at night when there'd be no fighting over the two machines the establishment felt adequate for a building that size.

Jerry picked up his ditty bag. As he started for the door, his phone chimed. Pulling it out, he saw a message from Max. He dropped the bag as he took a seat on the couch. The girl had keyed on the number for the hotel room, and as such, he wanted to give her his full attention.

Jerry opened the message and saw she'd attached a file. He clicked on it and waited for it to download. When the image appeared, it proved to be an incredible likeness of him sitting at the table at the Port Hope Hotel. The plate in front of him showed a likeness of the gigantic burger he'd somehow managed to finish. Jerry used his fingers to inspect the drawing, admiring her attention to detail. Jerry was impressed. Maxine Buchanan was a girl of many talents. He saved the photo and hit reply. *This is incredible. Great job, Max.* He hit send and watched Gunter, who seemed content with walking the room and sniffing everything in sight. Jerry yawned, closing his eyes as he waited for a reply.

A door slammed and Jerry opened his eyes, listening to whispered voices in the hall. Jerry reached for his gun, remembered he was in a hotel, and picked up his phone to check the time. The screen was blank. *It's dead.*

He pushed from the couch and saw daylight streaming in from a gap in the window. He scratched his head as he walked to the window and drew the curtains open. It took a moment for his brain to register that the sun was rising instead of setting. It made sense since it had been dark when he arrived. His room overlooked the parking lot. Jerry searched out his ride and then scanned the area for the black sedan. Not seeing it, he turned from the window, looked at the bed, and sighed. Gunter was stretched to his full length, sleeping with his head resting on one of the many pillows.

"Glad you enjoyed the bed, dog."

Gunter opened his eyes, yawned, then rolled to his back with his legs in the air and head cocked to the side.

Jerry laughed. "Excuse me for disturbing you."

Gunter's eyes remained closed, but the dog rewarded him with a tail wag.

If the clock on the nightstand was to be believed, it was 5:16 in the morning.

Jerry pulled his charger out of the bag and plugged in his phone. He waited for the power to show one percent, then powered it on, checking for messages. There was one from Max. It simply read *Thanks*.

Eyeing the laundry bag, he decided to check to see if the machines were in use. Jerry picked up the bag and turned to look at Gunter. "Don't mind me.

I'm just going down the hall. I don't have my phone with me, so don't bother trying to call."

Gunter groaned and rolled to his side but made no move to follow.

Jerry shook his head. "Some watchdog you are."

Jerry walked the length of the hall looking for the washing machines, then went to the stairwell. He took the stairs up to the next floor for no other reason than he chose to go up instead of down and walked the length of that hall as well. He'd just about given up when he saw a map of the building that showed the laundry to be on the first floor. The elevator opened just as he turned. Not one to miss an opportunity, Jerry stepped inside and pushed the button for the first floor. As the door slid closed, the hair on the back of Jerry's neck started to tingle. *Easy, McNeal. You're just freaking out because you put yourself in a vulnerable position. What were you thinking taking the elevator when you could have easily taken the stairs? You moved your car away from the pole so you couldn't get boxed in, and now you're inside a box with only one way out. Brilliant, Marine.*

Jerry ran a hand over his head and started to press the button for the second floor when Gunter appeared in the box next to him. The dog leaned into his leg and looked up at him with golden brown eyes. Jerry met the dog's gaze and Gunter wagged his tail. This time, the tail wag felt more like an apology for leaving him alone. Jerry ran his free hand over the dog's back and continued on to the first floor. The elevator jerked to a stop and the doors slid open. A man started to step in, saw Jerry, and moved to the side. As Jerry exited, he made eye contact with the desk clerk who'd checked him in the evening prior. The man's eyes grew wide and he turned, hurrying to the back office.

Jerry looked at Gunter. "Is it me, or is something up with that guy?"

Gunter replied with a low growl.

"I agree. We need to keep an eye on him."

Gunter licked his lips.

Jerry eyed the dog. "You wouldn't really eat him, would you?"

Gunter licked his lips a second time and lifted his muzzle to show a K-9 smile.

The room set aside for guest laundry was at the end of the hallway near the ice machine. There were four machines in total, two washing machines and two dryers – all were empty. Not one for sorting, Jerry dumped everything into the machine and tossed the yellow mesh ditty bag in on top of his clothes. He purchased a single box of detergent from the vending machine in the same room and added the contents to the washer. He selected the hot wash to get everything good and clean, then counted out enough change to pay for his wash and slid the metal slot forward to start the machine. Jerry looked at

Gunter and jabbed his thumb toward the machine. "I don't know why Sarge is so anti-laundry. There's nothing to it."

Gunter yawned his reply.

Jerry debated leaving the machine but figured he had enough time to grab something to eat. Gunter stayed at his side as he walked to the breakfast area. A woman wearing a white button-up chef's coat moved around the room, placing breakfast items around the counter. As Jerry stepped into the room, the woman glanced at the clock above the counter.

She wiped her forehead with the back of her hand, then puckered her lips and blew the hair from her face. "It's not ready just yet, but the coffee's ready. Help yourself."

Jerry nodded his head. "Much obliged."

The woman smiled and looked him over, her eyes settling on his boots. "Nice manners. You must be a cowboy."

Jerry chuckled and reached for a cup. "No, ma'am, just had a mother and grandmother. Both of which would have backhanded me if I answered any other way."

The woman smiled. "That's what's wrong with the world today. People are afraid of disciplining their kids. When I was young, my mom and dad thought nothing of beating the crap out of us kids if we did something wrong. We lost that. I see it all the time. A kid acts up, and the parent hands them their phone to pacify them. Can you imagine your parents rewarding you for a temper tantrum?"

Jerry shook his head. "No, ma'am."

"And nobody talks to one another. They just sit there looking and laughing into their phone." The woman paused. "I'm sorry. You get me started, and I don't know where to stop. It's still a bit early, but everything is out. Go ahead and help yourself."

Jerry went to the counter, helping himself to scrambled eggs, biscuits as hard as hockey pucks, and a sausage patty. As he returned to his table, he noticed a man come through the front door of the building. Wearing blue jeans and a collared shirt, the man smiled at the clerk behind the desk and continued to the breakfast area, where he loaded a plate and took it to a table near one of the televisions. Leaving the plate on the table, the man returned for coffee, a carton of milk, and apple juice, and picked up one of the free newspapers on the way back to his table. While the man didn't do anything in particular to set off warning bells, something about him didn't feel right. Jerry positioned himself so he could keep an eye on the guy. He reached for his phone to take a photo of the man, then remembered he'd left his phone charging in his room.

The man took his time eating and returned to the breakfast bar on two occasions before deciding he'd had enough. Twenty minutes after his initial arrival, he rose, cleared his table, and pocketed a banana.

Placing the newspaper on the table where he'd found it, the guy walked directly to the front door. Jerry followed and stayed out of sight as he watched the guy get into an older Volvo and leave.

Jerry returned to the building in time to see the clerk look up and hurry to the back room. Jerry rolled his neck. *What's with that guy?* Jerry thought about asking the dude what his problem was, then decided it wasn't worth the trouble. *Some people are just weird.*

The washing machine had stopped by the time Jerry returned. He tossed his clothes into the dryer, added a few coins, and started the machine. Once again, he debated the wisdom of leaving his clothes unattended. *Get over yourself, McNeal. Who's going to want your jeans and skivvies?*

Realizing he was being too overprotective over his belongings, Jerry decided to return to the room for a quick shower. Even with Gunter by his side, he opted to take the stairs to the second floor. Walking to his room, he keyed on his room number, two-hundred-seven. The hairs on the back of his neck prickled. *Easy, McNeal. You're keying on Max, not a premonition.* Even though Jerry knew his inner voice was correct, he let the shepherd take the lead. If anything was wrong, the dog would know it. Jerry didn't stop to realize if there'd been something wrong, the dog would have already warned him of it. He used the card to open the door and waited a full beat before entering. Once inside, the feeling intensified. He scanned the room but didn't see anything amiss. Gunter sniffed the air then walked to the adjoining door, sniffing the carpet around the opening. Jerry walked to the door and tested the handle. *Locked.* Seeing that the door opened into his room, he motioned Gunter away and slid the large easy chair in front of it. He walked to the desk and tore a piece of paper from the pad. Folding it several times, he wedged it between the door and the frame.

Jerry rooted in the seabag and pulled out a change of clothes and his shaving kit. He sat everything on the sink in the bathroom and turned the water on in the shower. He started to undress and hesitated. Returning to the room, he went to the small wardrobe and pulled out his gun bag. He took a breath and opened it, peeking inside. Seeing everything in order, he replaced it.

Jerry ran a hand over his head. *You're getting paranoid in your old age, McNeal.* Jerry started for the shower and hesitated once more, deciding to check his phone for messages. As he unplugged it, his phone lit up, something that should not have happened as he'd made sure to turn it off before leaving for breakfast so it would charge faster. Jerry looked toward the adjoining door once more. The paper was still there.

He picked up his pistol from the table and took it into the bathroom. The dog might have his back, but he wanted to make sure his front was covered as well.

Chapter Six

While not happy with the knowledge someone had been in his room, the shower helped settle him. That Gunter hadn't reacted left him questioning if he'd actually turned off his cell. That the guns were left untouched further led him to believe perhaps he'd been mistaken. Jerry dressed and decided it was time to hit the streets in search of Rosie Freeman.

Jerry tucked his pistol into the back of his pants and double-checked the room. The paper was still wedged in the door, and he'd moved his seabag into the closet. He thought about leaving his gun bag where it had been but decided against it. While he managed to decrease his worry, something still tugged at the back of his neck.

Gunter stayed at his side, matching him step for step as they descended the stairs. Jerry thought about stopping and having a chat with the desk clerk, but a woman now stood behind the desk. She looked up from the computer as he approached but made no move to leave.

She smiled her greeting. "Checking out?"

"Actually, I was hoping to stay a couple more

nights."

"Okay. What's your room number?"

Jerry decided to play a hunch. "Two-oh-seven. The night clerk said it was the only one available."

The clerk frowned. "Kenny said that?"

"It was late. I was tired and may have misunderstood him." *Not likely.*

"Okay, good. Because we have plenty of rooms if you'd like to change."

Jerry thought about it for a moment. "No, I think I'll stay right where he put me. It's a nice room, and I didn't hear any noise from the other room. That reminds me, my sister is coming up for the weekend. Is the adjoining room next to me vacant?"

The clerk drummed the keys. "No, it looks to be rented for the next five days."

Jerry started to walk away and hesitated. "Maybe my sister came in early. I told her to ask for the room next to me. Could you check to see who's in the room next to mine?"

The clerk drummed on the keys once more. "What's your sister's name?"

"Betty Lou Cobb?" Okay, so he'd given his grandmother's name. It was the only one he could think of off the top of his head.

The clerk shook her head. "No, sir, the person's last name isn't Cobb."

Jerry placed his hand under his chin and drummed his lips with his index finger. "She said she might be bringing a date, but for the life of me, I can't remember the guy's name."

The clerk looked from side to side. "I'm not supposed to give out guest information, but maybe a last name will tell you if it is your sister's friend."

Jerry smiled a wide smile. "If I heard it, I would know if it's him."

"Jefferies."

Just a little more, McNeal. "That's it, Jefferies. I knew I'd know it if I heard it. Now to remember the first name, so I don't seem like a jerk. I've met the guy two times. You'd think I'd remember his name. I like to have a drink or seven, and I was drinking both times we met."

The clerk giggled and nodded her understanding. She looked back at the screen. "His name's Alfred."

Jerry winked. "That's it. You're a lifesaver. Hey, if you see them, don't tell them I know they're here."

Her smile faded. "And risk losing my job? No way!"

Good girl. "Great. It will be a big surprise."

Jerry was nearly out the door when he remembered his laundry. The dryer was stopped, but the washing machine was going. Jerry's clothes were each neatly folded and tucked into the ditty bag, all of which now sat on top of the machine. Jerry heaved a sigh and looked down at Gunter. "Well, boy, I guess there are good people left in the world."

Gunter jumped up, placing his front paws on the washer. He leaned in and pressed his nose to the bag. Lifting his head, he bared his teeth and gave a throaty growl.

Jerry plucked the bag from the machine. He laughed. “What, you don’t like strangers touching my skivvies?”

Gunter replied with a squeaky yawn.

Jerry hoisted the bag over his shoulder. He debated taking it back to the room and then decided against it. Gunter stayed at his side as they walked across the parking lot. Out of his peripheral vision, Jerry saw the black sedan he’d eyed the night before.

Gunter tensed and emitted a low growl. Jerry switched the gun bag to his right hand and used his left to settle the dog. Jerry used his key fob to start the Durango. “Easy, boy. I know they are there, but so far, they don’t know I know. I’ve got a plan. When I open the door, there will be no time for dawdling. I need you in and out of my way.”

Gunter took the need for a speedy retreat to heart as he disappeared and reappeared in the passenger seat wearing his K-9 vest. Jerry smiled. *Man, I love that dog.*

Jerry increased his stride, got in his SUV, and closed the door. He pulled the seatbelt around, pressed the brake, and pushed the start button to engage the engine all in one smooth motion. As the sedan moved to block his way, Jerry looked over each shoulder, put the Durango into reverse, and backed over the curb – turning so that the Durango was facing the opposite direction of the sedan. He switched to drive and sped off before the sedan cleared the parking lot.

Jerry made several turns, checking his rearview mirror as he went. After several moments with no sighting, he rolled his neck and glanced at Gunter. "Why is it I feel like a criminal hiding from the law?"

Gunter disappeared and reappeared. Jerry started laughing and nearly drove off the road. Gunter now had an orange bandana tied around his neck, and his police vest had been replaced with a leather vest complete with a Harley emblem. As soon as Jerry quit laughing, he looked to the roof and addressed the unknown. "You do know that is profiling, right?"

Gunter bared his teeth in a K-9 grin and stuck his head through the window of the SUV. Jerry blew out a long breath. The moment of levity was precisely what he needed to refocus on the seriousness of his mission.

Jerry cleared his mind, focusing his thoughts on Rosie Freeman. He drove through the heart of Salem, trying to get a lead on the woman. He felt a pull and turned left onto Bentley Street. To his surprise, the energy pull he'd felt was gone. Bentley was a one-way, so he continued up the street and circled back around to Essex Street. Pausing where he'd felt the pull, he felt nothing of the energy he'd felt only a moment prior. Jerry drummed his fingers on the steering wheel. "She was here a moment ago. It's as if she just disappeared."

Gunter groaned.

Jerry realized what he'd said. "I deserved that."

A black sedan cruised by. Jerry looked in the window, relaxing when he saw the windows weren't tinted, nor was the driver – a woman who looked to be in her seventies – looking in his direction. Jerry ran a hand over his head. It wasn't like him to be this paranoid. This thought elicited another groan from the dog. Not for the first time, Jerry thought about telling the dog to stay out of his head. But minor nuisances aside, Jerry liked being able to communicate with the K-9 without speaking. "Okay, not since meeting you. Is that what you want to hear?"

Gunter wagged his tail and responded with a puppy-like yip.

Jerry smiled and turned onto Bentley for a second time. Still not getting a hit on Rosie, he followed the street through to Essex Street, then continued on until he found a parking lot and backed into a space amongst a dozen other cars and SUVs behind Nathanial's Restaurant. "We will leave the Durango here and take a walk around town."

Gunter looked up and tilted his head.

Jerry scratched the dog behind the ear. "I'm not scared. I'm being cautious. Besides, we work alone. Can you imagine trying to catch a lead with those two guys hanging around? If they do have the room next to us, we'll see them soon enough. Let's head back over to Bentley Street. I'm pretty sure I got a hit on something over there."

The walk over to Bentley Street wasn't bad, but after seeing several joggers, Jerry found he wished himself among them. He tried to recall the last time he went running and realized it was when he'd shadowed Alex during the zombie run. He remembered Gunter showing up looking like a zombie dog and laughed out loud. Gunter tilted his head in Jerry's direction.

Jerry stopped and looked at the dog. "Yes, I'm laughing at you."

At that, Gunter jumped up, placing his paws on Jerry's chest. Jerry smiled and roughed the K-9's fur as the dog licked the side of his face. Jerry motioned him down, wiping his face with his shirt. "Enough of that, Dude. We have work to do."

Gunter dipped into a playful bow. Jerry shook his head. "Sorry, boy, it's not playtime. We are here to find Rosie Freeman, remember?"

Undeterred, Gunter lunged at Jerry, then retreated. As Jerry began walking, the dog repeated the action.

Jerry dodged to the left just as Gunter reached

him. "What in the world has gotten into you today?"

Gunter dipped into a bow for a second time, barking and wagging his tail. Jerry raced toward the dog with his hands in the air. Enjoying the moment, Gunter took off circling as he kept just out of reach. When the dog finally allowed Jerry to catch him, he and Gunter were both out of breath. The only difference, Jerry's tongue was not hanging from his mouth.

"It's good to see you've taken my advice to heart."

Jerry looked to see Granny by his side. "Are you the one that put him up to that?"

"I didn't put him up to anything. I suspect he felt how tense you were and decided to take your mind off it." Granny fell into step beside him. "You were always too serious when you were young. Even when you were a boy, you seemed older than your age. I wish you'd had a dog when you were a boy."

Jerry stifled a sigh. He'd never thought himself missing out on anything, but having enjoyed Gunter's company over the last several months, he had to agree that perhaps he'd missed out. "Dogs didn't like me."

"This one seems to."

Jerry glanced at Gunter, who had taken advantage of Granny being here and now walked ahead of Jerry with his nose to the ground sniffing everything in his path. "Gunter is one of a kind."

"You know that isn't true." Granny tilted her head and raised an eyebrow.

Jerry raised his hand. "Don't go getting any ideas. One dog is quite enough."

Granny looped her arm in his. "Don't be so sure, Jerry. You have a big heart and are capable of so much more love than this."

Instantly, an image of Holly came to mind.

Granny tightened her hold on his arm. "Who's that?"

Crap. Jerry quickly pushed the image aside. "Nobody."

"She didn't look like a nobody."

Jerry watched as Gunter, leading by several dog lengths, turned onto Bentley Street – the same street Jerry had keyed on earlier. He rolled his neck in response to Granny's comment.

"See, I was right. She does mean something to you."

He had never been able to hide anything from the woman – not even when she was alive. "I thought there might have been a connection, but there wasn't. Not on her end anyway."

"I could put in a good word for you."

"NO!" Jerry patted his grandmother's arm and lowered his tone. "I'm sorry I yelled. But please don't. Holly has my contact information. If she wanted to get ahold of me, she knows how."

"I don't see what would be wrong with a little

nudge."

"It's simple. If I'm going to connect with her or anyone else, I want it to be natural. I don't want to go through life wondering if the woman likes me for me or because of the nudge."

Granny stopped in her tracks. "You think my nudging her would somehow put a love spell on her?"

Jerry didn't answer.

The woman laughed. "Just because we are in a town known for its witchcraft doesn't make it so. I wouldn't be casting a spell – I would be whispering your name in the wind. I can assure you there's nothing dubious about that."

Jerry glanced at the muted grey building Gunter had keyed on, then turned his attention back to his grandmother. "I appreciate the offer, but it's still a no from me. Understood?"

"We'll see."

"No, we'll see. I want you to promise."

"We'll talk later. You have more pressing matters to attend to."

Jerry threw his hands up. "What could be more important than asking you to stay out of my love life?" She disappeared without answering just as a door slammed. Jerry turned and ran a hand over his head. A city police officer walked directly toward him. With his right hand resting on the butt of his pistol, it was apparent this wasn't a social call.

Chapter Seven

Jerry kept his hands in clear view and heaved a frustrated sigh – he knew Fred and Barney wanted to continue their previous conversation with him, but this was getting ridiculous. It was harassment, plain and simple. Furthermore, he would file a grievance if he ever found out who the men worked for. Jerry forced a smile. “Something I can help you with, officer?”

The officer walked a few more steps before stopping. “I was going to ask you the same thing. We’ve had multiple complaints of a guy fitting your description walking up and down the street waving his arms and talking to himself.”

Crap. Jerry liked it better when he thought Fred and Barney were the ones having him brought in. At least that would have meant an interrogation room versus a padded cell. *Let’s see you talk your way out of this, McNeal.* Jerry read the man’s name badge – *Tanton.* Jerry looked the man in the eye. “I have ID.”

Jerry heard a car pull up behind him and knew it was another officer, as the street he was on was a one-way road in the opposite direction, reinforced by the fact that Gunter alerted but didn't move into a protective stance. The problem at hand was when he moved to retrieve his wallet, the officer behind him would see the handle of his pistol.

Tanton kept his hand close to his gun. "Bring it out slow and easy."

Jerry closed his eyes for a moment. *Come on, McNeal, think like a cop.* Opening his eyes, he stretched his arms further and sank to his knees. *This better work.* "Brother, I'm a Pennsylvania State Trooper. I have a gun."

Tanton pulled his weapon and nodded to the officer behind him. Jerry felt, more than heard, the man come up behind him.

Gunter's ears pivoted. He alerted and licked his lips.

Easy boy; the man's just doing his job.

Gunter's tail lowered slightly, but he continued to keep watch.

"The gun's in my waistband." He'd no sooner uttered the words than the gun was pulled free.

Tanton looked at Jerry. "Now, let's see that ID."

Jerry lowered his right hand and pulled his wallet from his jeans. "I'm going to lower my left hand to get my ID."

The officer nodded his approval.

Jerry reached inside, pulled his license free, and held it in the air. Within seconds, the ID was pulled from between his fingers.

"Clamp your hands behind your back."

Jerry did as told, breathing easier when the officer holstered his pistol. Several moments passed before the second officer returned. Placing a hand under Jerry's elbow, the man helped him to his knees. Jerry turned to thank him. To his surprise, the officer wasn't a man but a petite blonde with amazing blue eyes. Her nametag read T. Burnes. Jerry wondered what the T stood for. "Tiffany" came to mind. *Yep, she looks like a Tiffany. Soft and sweet.*

"He's who he said he is. He is not very good at his job, though. According to dispatch, the yahoo lost his badge."

Okay, maybe not so soft or sweet.

Tanton looked him up and down. "What did you do to lose your badge?"

Burnes laughed and shook her head. "No, he actually lost it. That and his trooper ID."

Tanton raised an eyebrow. "You're kidding."

"Nope." Burnes handed him his ID, caught him staring, and smiled. "What's the matter? Don't they have women police officers in your state?"

They do, but not ones as pretty as you. Don't say it, Jer. Before he could respond, Tanton beat him to the punch.

"Sure, they do, Burnes, but not any as pretty as you." The man winked and turned his attention back to Jerry. "Okay, so you're a cop. That doesn't account for you talking to yourself. A man goes around doing that, and we think maybe he's not right in the head. That or drunk. Tell me you're not stupid enough to be drinking with a weapon on your hip."

Jerry ran his hand over his head and made a mental note to ask Seltzer to come up with a different cover story. "I'm neither drunk nor stupid. I'll be happy to submit to a sobriety test, but you'll have to take my word on the stupid part."

Tanton shook his head. "You don't seem drunk to me. Still, I have to ask what you were doing. Don't say 'nothing' because we got more than one call of you walking back and forth talking to yourself."

The truth – or what would be construed as it – would come out sooner or later. Jerry opted for sooner. "I'm looking into Rosie Freeman's disappearance."

Tanton exchanged glances with Burnes. "What do you know about Rosie Freeman?"

That neither cop asked who Rosie Freeman was led Jerry to believe they'd both worked the case or heard about it during shift change-over briefings. Either way, they were aware of the woman. "Nothing yet. I was trying to get a reading on her when you showed up."

"Get a reading? What's that supposed to mean?"

No guts, no glory, Jer. Anyone doing any amount of digging will know what you're all about.

"I'm a psychic. I was trying to channel Rosie to get a lead on her whereabouts and maybe learn something about her killer."

Burnes spoke up. "People go missing all the time. What makes you so sure she's dead?"

"It's just a hunch at the moment, but if I'm right, and I'm pretty sure I am, we'll know soon enough."

"You're pretty cocky for a guy who can't even find his badge and ID."

"Like I said, it's a hunch. Am I free to go?"

Burnes looked at Tanton. "Yeah, but you're going to have to play your hunches somewhere else. The residents on this street have already made it clear they don't want you here."

Jerry didn't mind leaving since he hadn't picked up anything on Rosie since the initial pull. What he didn't like was being told he wasn't free to walk down the city street even though he hadn't done anything wrong. How many times had he issued the same warning to individuals in the guise of doing his job? When he was on the force, the warning felt justified. At the moment, he was having trouble recalling what law took away a person's right to be treated fairly. *Don't be stupid, McNeal. They are only looking out for your personal safety. The only reason you aren't in cuffs is because they believed your lie.*

Gunter must have picked up on Jerry's inner turmoil, as the dog currently had hold of his pant leg, tugging him in the opposite direction. Jerry motioned for him to stop. Gunter tucked his tail and released his hold. Jerry looked over Tanton's shoulder, watching as a black Lincoln SUV pulled onto the street. The driver waited half a beat before putting the SUV into reverse and backing out once more. By now, anyone looking for him would know of his whereabouts. Anyone, including Fabel, who Jerry knew had a way of knowing when his name popped up on official channels.

Jerry nodded his agreement. He walked to the house Gunter had keyed on and glanced up at the second-floor window. He started toward the house.

Tanton called out to him. "McNeal?"

Jerry turned.

"I thought you said you were leaving?"

"I did. I just didn't say when."

***

Not only had Jerry's comment gotten him a ride in the back of Tanton's police cruiser, but Jerry was currently sitting at a table in a windowless room with Gunter lying at his side. The dog appeared miffed at him. Every now and then, the K-9 would lift an eyelid to make sure Jerry was still there.

After the sixth such exchange, Jerry shook his head. He started to chastise the dog but saw the two-way mirror and reconsidered. Not for the first time, Jerry was glad he hadn't ordered Gunter to stay out of his head. *Stop acting so disappointed in me.*

You're my bodyguard, not my nanny.

Gunter opened his eyes and yawned a condescending yawn.

Before Jerry could respond, the door opened. The men he knew as Fred and Barney came in and sat at the table across from him. They wore black suits, and Barney carried a cardboard holder with three paper cups.

Barney took one out and slid it across the table. "You do like your coffee black, right?"

Jerry took the cup and removed the lid, replacing it to his liking.

Barney frowned. "You don't trust me?"

Jerry smiled. "I don't trust the cup. Why they insist on putting the lid on with the spout touching the seam is beyond me. You can't take a drink without it spilling."

Barney lifted his cup, turning it from side to side before taking a drink. Jerry resisted an "I told you so" when the dark liquid trickled from the gap between the lid and the cup.

Fred secured his own lid before taking a taste. "You're a smart guy, McNeal. How come you allowed yourself to get arrested?"

"I wasn't arrested."

Fred lowered his cup. "Looks arrested to me. Don't it to you, Barn?"

Barney nodded his head.

"What was it you said to me in New York? No

Miranda, no arrest."

"They didn't read you your rights?"

"Nope. But I get the feeling you already know this."

"You put a lot of stock in those feelings of yours, don't you?"

"Enough to know it wouldn't take long for the two of you to walk through that door."

Barney chuckled, and Fred shot him a warning look.

"How'd you know we were in town?"

Jerry drummed his fingers on the table. "You first. What were you hoping to find in my room?"

Barney choked on the coffee he was in the process of drinking.

Fred sat back in his chair. "What makes you think we were?"

"I had a feeling." Jerry leaned back, mirroring his actions. "Which I followed up on. It seems you are in the room next to mine. You are one Mr. Alfred Jefferies, are you not? And let's not forget the black town car that tried to block me in when I was leaving the hotel."

Fred turned to Barney. "Remind me to have them add darker tint to the windows."

"Actually, the sedan was more of a guess than a feeling. But it's good to know Fabel's goons don't know where I'm staying just yet."

"Fabel's in town?"

"His goons are. I expect he won't be far behind."

"Where'd you see them."

"Bentley Street. They pulled in then turned around."

"That's why you decided to get yourself arrested?"

Jerry shook his head. "I'm not arrested, remember? But yes, that's why I agreed to come along. Either way, I knew I was going for a ride. I figured this to be the safest bet."

"How do you know it was Fabel's guys? Could be someone turned, saw the cop cars, and changed their mind."

Jerry met his gaze. "It was Fabel's guy."

"You got any proof? A license plate? Description of the driver?"

"Nope. Just my gut feeling."

Fred looked at Barney. "Make some calls and see if you can get some intel on Fabel's whereabouts."

Barney got up and left without comment.

Fred smiled at Jerry. "If Fabel's in town. It might not be so bad having us as neighbors."

Jerry forced a smile. *Great, just what I need, more babysitters.*

Gunter, who'd been quietly taking it all in, groaned and rolled over to his side.

Chapter Eight

Jerry rubbed his hand across his face and felt stubble. Having shaved before leaving the motel, the fact that he had stubble meant it had to be after four. Jerry stood and walked to the two-way mirror and tapped on the glass. "I'm ready to leave now. No Miranda, no arrest. I'm pretty sure this is illegal, and I could own the station."

Jerry paced the room under Gunter's watchful eye. He turned away from the mirror and kept his voice low. "I don't think I like being on this side of the law."

Gunter lowered to the ground and covered his face with his paws.

The door clicked open. Gunter lifted his head, watching as Fred came into the room. He placed two foiled spears on the table in front of him.

Jerry eyed them suspiciously.

Fred nodded toward the table. "Corndogs."

Jerry reached for one of the spears. "What am I, seven?"

"They're from Boston Hotdog. I didn't know how you liked your dog, so I just went with the safe bet." Fred reached in his pocket and pulled out several packs of mustard, tossing them onto the table.

"I like my hot dogs in the kitchen they are cooked in and smothered in chili." Jerry unwrapped the foil. He started to take a bite and hesitated. "I'd like a lawyer."

Fred pulled up a chair. "There's no need for an attorney. You said yourself you're not under arrest."

"And yet, I've been in an interrogation room for close to seven hours." Jerry knew he could have demanded to leave at any point. Two things were keeping him here. First, he wanted to get confirmation that Fabel's goons were, in fact, onto him. Second, he still wanted to know who these two worked for.

Fred looked at his watch and cocked an eyebrow. "You're pretty good. Another one of your feelings?"

Jerry chuckled. "Hardly. I just know how long it takes me to have a five o'clock shadow."

Fred turned the chair around and sat with his arms resting on the back. "You're a hard man to figure out, McNeal."

"Why's that?"

"You know your rights, and yet it took you until now to ask for a lawyer. I told you you're not under arrest, yet you're not demanding to leave. Why?"

Jerry shrugged. "I'm cheap. I was waiting for you to buy me lunch."

Fred shook his head. "Nah, that isn't it."

Jerry ignored him. "Any hit on the DNA from Rita's ring?"

Another shake of the head. "This isn't television. You were a cop. Those things take time."

Jerry sat back in his chair. "Speaking of being a cop. You're not. Neither is that partner of yours. Yet you have free rein to come and go as you please. What's the deal?"

Fred rubbed his chin. "How about we trade questions? I'll go first. How is it you're able to find those women when no one else has been able to?"

"You've obviously read my file enough to know I'm psychic."

"Listen, McNeal. I'm prepared to stay with this as long as it takes. I'm just as prepared to give you the answers you want. But not until I get a straight answer. I know you're psychic. But I've been around enough clairvoyants to know there is more to it. I've also dealt with enough to know most who claim to be are selling snake oil."

"Which category do you think I fall into?"

Fred smiled a wide smile. "That is what I've been trying to establish."

Jerry got the feeling the guy wanted to believe him, but he also knew Fred was holding back. He studied the man sitting in front of him with a new set of eyes. *You want something. Something personal. There's a kid involved, but not your kid.*

Instantly, all animosity Jerry felt toward the guy dissipated. Jerry pushed the corndog aside and sighed. "Just how open-minded are you?"

Fred's face turned serious. "Try me and see."

Jerry glanced toward the two-way mirror. "Okay, but not here."

"You got a problem with police stations?"

Jerry gave a nod toward the mirror. "I have a problem not knowing who is standing on the other side of that glass listening to what is supposed to be a private conversation."

Fred sighed his acceptance. "Do you mind if my partner tags along?"

Not if you don't mind if mine comes. Jerry kept that last sentiment to himself. "Nope."

"Where do you want to go?"

Jerry smiled. "We'll discuss that once we get out of the building."

***

Fred sat in the passenger seat of the sedan and waited for Barney to climb behind the wheel. Fred turned and looked over the seat at Jerry. "Okay, McNeal, it's your show. Where to?"

"That place you got those dogs from around here?"

"Boston Hot Dog Company? Sure, what about it?"

Jerry made eye contact with Barney, who was staring at him through the rearview mirror. "They got beer?"

Barney looked to Fred, then glanced in the mirror once more. "Root beer."

"It'll do."

Fred gave the okay and faced forward once more as Barney put the sedan in drive and drove the short drive to their destination. Jerry wasn't sure what to expect of the place, but it wasn't the large three-story red brick building that loomed beside them when Barney pulled to the curb. Jerry noted the outside seating area and tagged Fred on the shoulder. "There's a free table. Get me a couple of chili dogs with onions, fries, and a root beer. Make sure to order Barney some fries, so he keeps his fingers out of mine. He and I are going to nab a table."

Fred frowned. "It's hot out. What's wrong with sitting inside?"

Jerry smiled, and Fred went inside without another word.

***

Fred waited until Jerry finished the second of what Fred had informed him were Carnival dogs and leveled a look at him. "You've finished your meal. It's time to talk."

Jerry ran a napkin over his mouth and tossed it in the bag along with the paper cartons the dogs came in. He nodded to the bank across the street. "See that tree?"

Both men looked. It was Fred who spoke. "The

one next to the street sign?"

"That's the one. What if I told you there is a man leaning against it smoking a pipe?"

Fred scrunched his eyes. "I'd say you have better vision than I do."

"What if I told you the man's dead, and what I'm actually seeing is his spirit."

To their credit, neither man laughed. Barney, however, did appear more skeptical. "So you just happened to pick a place that has a ghost standing in front of it?"

"Nope. There just happens to be a ghost standing in front of the place I picked."

Barney scratched his head. "Isn't that what I said?"

Jerry winked at Gunter, who was sitting next to him. "Here's the deal. We are in a place known for its hauntings. I can point out a half dozen spirits just from where I'm sitting."

Barney pointed. "Is she a ghost?"

Jerry looked to see an elderly woman navigating the crosswalk. "Have you ever seen a ghost before?"

Barney shook his head. "Not that I know of."

Jerry smiled. "Your streak continues. The woman's old, but she's as alive as the three of us."

Fred laughed as Barney frowned his disappointment. The older man turned serious once more. "It's one thing to say you see ghosts. It's another to prove it."

Barney bobbed his head. "The government says they've sent people to the moon, but there's no evidence to prove it."

Fred closed his eyes and sighed. "Now you've done it." Fred raised a hand to silence his partner. "This is not the time or place, partner."

Jerry looked across the table at Fred, who he was fairly sure would shoot him if he further provoked the man. "He does realize he works for the government, right?"

"Does he?"

"I thought we were past all of that."

"You said you see ghosts. You didn't show us any proof."

Jerry looked at Gunter lying on the sidewalk next to him. That the dog was so relaxed was a good sign, as it meant the men were close to being convinced.

Barney scanned the sidewalk. "Do you see any witches?"

Jerry rubbed his hand over his head and addressed his comment to Fred. "Where'd you get this guy?"

Fred shrugged. "Better answer him, or he won't be able to sleep tonight."

"I see the man by the tree, two women walking up the sidewalk toward him, and a horse."

Both men whipped their heads around. Barney's eyes were wide with amazement. "You're saying there are animal spirits? That's a load of bull."

Jerry nodded his confirmation and resisted looking at Gunter.

Barney stared off in the distance. "You said there are three women. Are any of them witches?"

"I guess they could be." *Great. The man doesn't believe Neil Armstrong walked on the moon, but he'll readily accept the probability of witches walking the streets of Salem.* Jerry held a hand up to settle the man. "Here's the thing, Barney. It's not like they are wearing black hats and riding brooms. I wouldn't know if the women are witches, were accused of being witches, or anything else about them."

"But it's plausible?"

Jerry rolled his neck and laced his hands together to stop from strangling the man. He was supposed to be looking for the victim of a serial killer, and he was playing twenty questions with a man who was smart enough to be in whatever secret handshake club he was in, yet sounded like a total flake. Jerry blew out a sigh. Fun was fun, but he'd been distracted far too long.

"Am I to understand you can not only see the spirits, but you can speak to them as well?" Fred asked, bringing him from his musings. Though the man's demeanor hadn't changed, there was something about his energy that emitted a hopeful flare.

"That's exactly what I'm saying."

"And they can talk to you too?" Barney clarified. Though the man seemed eager to hear the answer, gone was the childish exuberance from moments earlier.

Jerry looked at the man with a new set of eyes, wondering if he'd been played. Something told him he was, and Jerry had taken the bait, hook, line, and sinker. "I can. And something tells me the whole moon thing was a skit you two have acted out before."

Fred shrugged. "He's floated a few theories, but that's as far as it goes."

Jerry stood, eager to be finished with the two. "You gentlemen may not have anything better to do than screw with a man's life, but I have a crime to solve. There is a serial killer out there killing women, even if you two clowns are too foolish to realize it."

"Give it to him."

Jerry hesitated as Barney pulled an envelope from the inside pocket of his blazer.

Jerry looked at the envelope, which had his name typewritten across it. "What's this?"

"The reward for information leading to the whereabouts of Rita Wadsworth. Unless you don't want it. The way I hear it, you've got more money than you know what to do with. That's why you gave what Fabel paid you to the girl and her mother, right?"

"Max earned every penny of that reward."

Fred glanced at Barney. "The girl, she's psychic too?"

Jerry wasn't comfortable with their sudden interest in Max. "Let's leave Max and her mother out of whatever this is."

Fred held up his hands. "We have no interest in either of them."

Jerry returned to his seat. "Unless I don't do whatever it is you want me to."

"I didn't say that." Fred turned to Barney. "Did you hear me say that?"

Barney shook his head. "I most definitely did not hear you say that."

Fred pointed to the envelope. "Look inside."

Jerry opened the envelope, eyed the amount, and swallowed.

"You're not going to give that one away too, are you?"

"No, I found Rita on my own." Jerry folded the envelope and stuck it inside his back pocket. To his left, he heard Gunter yawn a squeaky yawn. "Sorry."

Fred turned his head. "What?"

Jerry cleared his throat. "I said I'm keeping it."

Fred slid a card across the table. "My personal cell. If you need anything, call."

"Does that mean you believe me?"

"Let's say we want to believe you."

"What's that supposed to mean?"

"You've made a few mistakes. You still have to prove yourself."

"I don't have to prove myself to anyone." Jerry pushed off from the wooden seat. He took about fifteen steps before his curiosity got the better of him. He turned around, retracing his path. "What mistakes?"

Fred held out a hand, and Barney placed a ten-dollar bill in his palm.

Crap. Once again, he'd played right into their trap. Jerry looked down at Gunter, who had never moved from his resting place. *Good going, McNeal. Even the dog knew you'd come back.* Jerry ran his hand over his head. "What mistakes?"

Barney's cell rang. Fred waved him off. "Take your call. I've got this. Back in New York, when you told us about Ashley Fabel, you said she died in 2018, further saying she died three months after your friend Patti. She was your friend, right?"

"I'd known her when we were young. If you want to make something of it, don't. Part of the reason Patti's spirit came to me is because we were friends." It was true, and he was okay with that. What he wasn't okay with was that he'd made such a rookie mistake as getting the dates wrong. He blew it off. "So, I got a date wrong. Dead is dead. You said mistakes. What were the others?"

"Drawing attention to yourself."

"I don't understand."

"This morning. All of this could have been avoided if you'd had earbuds or a Bluetooth hanging from your ear. You could have simply held your phone to your ear and pretended to be talking to your grandmother."

"I was."

"Was what?"

"Talking to my grandmother."

Fred pulled out a notebook. "It says here your grandmother is dead."

Jerry cocked an eyebrow. "Your point?"

Fred smiled and slid Jerry's gun and an outdated Bluetooth earpiece across the table. "Use this."

Jerry placed his pistol in the waist of his jeans and picked up the Bluetooth, turning it back and forth. "This thing's a dinosaur."

"It can be seen. That's all you need. Now people will just think you're too cheap to spring for a new one."

"Anything else?"

Fred stood and started for his car. "Just one."

"Which was?"

"When you were telling about all the ghosts in the area, you neglected to mention your dog."

Jerry glanced at Gunter, then back to Fred. "How'd you know about Gunter?"

Fred collected the trash from the table. He looked toward Gunter, then tossed Jerry his keys. "Go do what it is you do, and we'll talk later."

Jerry wanted to tell Fred he didn't want to wait until later, that he wanted everything cleared up now, but he didn't want the man to see how unsettled he was. Playing it cool, Jerry started to walk away. He took several steps before pivoting back around. "Hey?"

Fred looked in his direction. "Yeah?"

"What did your partner find out about Fabel and his goons?"

Fred shoved the bag in the garbage can. "Absolutely nothing. Keep your wits about you, McNeal. So far, there's no evidence of them being in town."

Chapter Nine

Jerry was a block away before realizing he'd left without getting the information he wanted. Though Fred and Barney knew his secrets, he was no closer to knowing who the men worked for. He'd insisted they leave the police station so he would have the upper hand, and all he'd succeeded in doing was feed them more information.

He'd left thinking to walk back over to Bentley Street and finish what he'd started, only he was growing increasingly angry with each step. Jerry stopped. Gunter paused, cocking his head toward him as if trying to gauge Jerry's next move.

"Okay, this stops now. I've got a perfectly good vehicle, and I'm walking around hiding from someone who may not even be in town." *Oh, he's in town, McNeal. It's not just a hunch; you can feel it in your veins.* Jerry rubbed his hand over his head. "Even so, why am I letting the man dictate my actions? I'm walking around town with nothing more than a pistol when I've got enough firepower in the Durango to start a small war."

An image of Arnold Schwarzenegger came to

mind. Jerry laughed. "This isn't make-believe. I'm sure even Fred and Barney would have an issue with me shooting up the whole town. Okay, so I won't use the guns. I know karate. I can hold my own. Not to mention I travel with my own stealth security system. Isn't that right, Gunter?"

Gunter jumped up, placed his paws on Jerry's chest, and growled a menacing growl.

Jerry patted the dog on his shoulders. "That's what I'm talking about. It's time for me to stop acting like a wuss." Jerry realized he'd spoken out loud. He motioned Gunter down and pulled the Bluetooth from his pocket. Placing it in his ear, he pulled out his phone and used it to get directions to Nathanial's Restaurant, where he'd left his Durango.

It was nearly seven p.m. when Jerry made his way back to Bentley Street, driving the length of it, then circling around the block and driving up the street once more. Even though he was in his Durango, he had the Bluetooth stuck in his ear canal in case anyone questioned his sanity. The device was not only worthless but also unnecessary, as the spirit he was searching for was not there. As a matter of fact, he hadn't seen any spirits on the street.

Jerry pulled the earpiece from his ear and placed it in the cupholder. He looked over at Gunter, who had his head stuck through the glass. "Got any ideas?"

Gunter made no move to answer, so Jerry circled and headed toward the water. He found a spot where he could stay in the SUV and still see the water. Though he hadn't planned it, he could see the replica of the tall sailing ship *Friendship of Salem* as well. Jerry parked and let the Durango idle as he tapped the dash and dialed Seltzer's number.

"Jerry, my boy, I was wondering when you'd call. Seems you've got yourself into a little trouble."

That Seltzer already knew he'd been picked up didn't surprise him. It was he who kept Jerry in the system in the first place. "I'm out, but we have to work on a new strategy."

"What's wrong with the one we have?"

"Besides making me look like a total buffoon?"

"Okay. I'll try and think of something. Anything else going on?"

"Everything and nothing."

"That sounds convoluted."

Jerry saw a German shepherd sniffing the grassy area in front of the Durango and checked the passenger seat. Empty. Jerry tapped his fingers on the steering wheel, trying to decide not only where to start but how much to tell. Jerry let out a sigh. Not only did he not want to lie to the man, he wanted him to know what was going on in case things went awry.

"Did your friend find out anything about the two men I was telling you about?"

"Seems your friends didn't leave a lot of clues."

Jerry pictured the cameras he'd seen in the bar. "The video wasn't any help?"

"They were wiped clean. Supposedly, there was a malfunction, and everything had to be reset."

"That's pretty convenient."

"What about the waitress who was working that night?"

"Said she was so overwhelmed with tables and couldn't recall a thing."

Jerry chuckled. "It was after dinnertime, and there were only three tables in use."

"It means they got to her. Scared her into keeping quiet."

"Nah, she didn't seem the type to get scared. Most likely, they paid her enough to keep her mouth shut. Someone offers someone enough money, they are going to clam up. I understand that. The thing I don't understand is who they are hiding from and why."

"Are you sure they are cops?"

"Cops, no. But they are in with some super top-secret double-handshake club."

"How can you be so sure? They haven't produced any badges. Maybe they just want you to think they are."

"They are with some organization. They've had me in an interrogation room most of the day." Jerry braced for the man's outrage.

"Why didn't you call me?" Seltzer's tone was ice cold, and Jerry knew the man was reaching for his ever-present pack of gum to calm his rage.

"These guys don't play by the rules. I ask for a lawyer, and they tell me I'm not under arrest. I ask for a phone call, and they ignore my request." Jerry thought about telling him they'd searched his room but didn't want to give his former sergeant reason to jump on a plane.

"If I get my hands on those two jokers…"

"I can handle those two." *Sure you can, McNeal. That's why you don't know any more about them than you did before.* "I think we've bridged some kind of gap."

"What makes you think that?"

"Well, for one thing, when they turned me loose, they gave me back my gun."

"Maybe they're hoping you'll shoot someone so they can have a legitimate reason to lock you up?"

So much for a meeting of the minds. Leave it to Seltzer to come up with a theory he himself hadn't thought of. Jerry ran a hand over his head to calm his nerves. "I get the feeling Fred wants something from me."

"You sure?"

"I was until a few moments ago."

"Any idea what?"

"It feels personal."

"Personal how?"

"Like there's a kid involved. I get the impression he's trying to decide if he can trust me. In fact, he all but said that very thing." Jerry thought about telling him what Fred had said about his mistakes but decided against it. Feeling like a buffoon was one thing. Giving evidence to prove it to be true was another. "There's something else. I told them about seeing ghosts."

"That's a big leap of faith. What did they say?"

Jerry considered telling him about Barney's performance, then pressed on. "I got the impression they already knew about that."

"What makes you think that?"

"Because they knew what I didn't tell them."

"Which was?"

"They knew about Gunter." That Jerry could count on one hand the number of people who knew of the dog's existence was troubling.

"I wouldn't worry about that too much. They go blabbing about the dog, deny it, and those two will lose their credibility."

Jerry looked at Gunter, who was still tracing an invisible path. That they couldn't do anything to hurt the dog wasn't the point. It was the fact that he currently felt betrayed. Everyone who knew about Gunter was people he previously thought he could count on.

Seltzer brought him out of his musings. "So, how do you gain his trust?"

"Keep on doing what I'm doing. Find Rosie Freeman and lead authorities to where she's buried."

A man dressed in old-world garb appeared just outside Jerry's SUV. Even before the man stuck his head through the glass, Jerry knew the man to be long dead. Jerry lifted his index finger, wagging it from side to side, letting the spirit know his behavior was unacceptable. The spirit pulled his head free and stood looking into the glass.

"You haven't found her yet? That's rare for you."

"I've been a little preoccupied." Jerry took a deep breath. Seltzer wasn't going to like what he was getting ready to say. "Fabel's goons are in the area."

"Son of a…"

Jerry cut him off. "It's under control."

"That's a load of baloney, and you know it."

It was, but Jerry wasn't about to let his former sergeant know it. He decided to bring out the big dogs. Literally. "Gunter and I have everything under control."

Gunter looked up, saw the spirit, and trotted toward the Durango. Instead of disappearing, the man started running toward the ship, which was moored halfway down the grassy pier. Gunter followed closely behind. From Jerry's point of view, the dog was merely following the man, but the way the apparition kept looking over his shoulder showed he was not in on the game.

Jerry shook his head. *How is this my life*? "I've got to go."

"Problem?"

"You wouldn't believe me if I told you."

"Fabel?" The worry was evident in the man's tone.

"Not unless he's dead. I'll call you tomorrow." Jerry disconnected the call and turned off the SUV. He opened the door and whistled for Gunter, who did a wide turn and headed in his direction. Behind him, the ghostly body stopped and shook his fist before ultimately disappearing.

Jerry rolled his neck. He was pretty sure the vessel was closed for tours by this hour. Even if not, he figured it wasn't anything that couldn't wait another day. The truth of the matter was he wanted to give the fellow time to cool off before seeing what it was he wanted.

Gunter returned, looking rather pleased with himself. Jerry pointed his finger at the dog. "You are supposed to have my back. Not cause me more problems."

Gunter whined his apology, lowered his head, and tucked his tail between his legs. Jerry felt instant remorse for having scolded the dog. He drummed on his upper chest with his hands. Gunter sprang to life, jumping up and licking Jerry's face, letting him know all was forgiven.

***

As soon as Jerry placed the Durango into gear, he felt a pull leading him back to Washington Street. He parked, and Gunter remained plastered against his left leg as Jerry made his way to Essex Street Pedestrian Mall. The mall area was bustling with people visiting the shops. Jerry and Gunter wove through the crowd, each feeling the pull continuing until they stopped facing a small gathering of people standing in front of a red brick building. A woman dressed in black stood on the steps of the building, speaking to those standing before her. A matronly woman with a wide girth, she spoke in enthusiastic tones, telling the history of the building. Jerry instantly recognized it to be one of the city's many walking ghost tours. He scanned the small gathering of eager listeners, further noting how each of the watchers stood, hanging on the woman's every word. She pointed to one of the upper windows and told how it was said the mistress of the house still walked the house at night. The wind blew through the open window, the curtains moved, and a few in the crowd gasped. Jerry looked at Gunter to see if the dog had keyed on something he couldn't see. The dog gave no sign that he had.

Smiling at the novelty of wishing for a ghostly sighting, Jerry moved on, his thoughts on his own ghostly companion at his side. Gunter moved with him, stepping as he stepped, and Jerry got the impression they were somehow connected by an invisible lead. The further they moved away from the small group, the more anxious Jerry felt until he finally gave in to the feeling and circled back to find the group. They were on the move.

Jerry slowed his pace, aiming to leave a large enough gap so that the woman giving the tour wouldn't admonish him for joining the tour without paying. He stayed near the edge of the adjoining building, watching. Once again, the small gathering stopped in front of a dark brown house. The woman leading the tour lowered her voice as she spoke. For a moment, Jerry thought she'd done so to keep him from hearing but soon realized she'd merely done so to draw the people closer. She told a tragic story of love and how the young woman was so upset that her husband didn't return from the war that she'd gone on a hunger strike and subsequently starved herself to death.

"It is said," the woman whispered, "that she can be seen sitting in that swing over there waiting for her lover to return to her." As she spoke, the woman pointed to the swing, and everyone turned to look. The crowd sighed a collective sigh when the swing proved to be empty. As the group moved on, Jerry noticed a man in a ballcap lingering behind. Jerry figured the man was hoping the ghost would appear once everyone left. He must have felt Jerry watching him as he turned, staring at Jerry. Though the curve in the silhouette was subtle, Jerry realized he'd been mistaken. The person was not a man but a lanky woman wearing a ballcap. Though her hair was pulled up under the cap, there was enough of it hanging loose around her face that Jerry knew it to be red.

He took a step forward, then another, and still another as Gunter moved cautiously alongside him. When Jerry was close enough to speak without raising his voice, he smiled. "Hello, Rosie. My name is Jerry McNeal. I've been looking all over for you."

Rosie's eyes grew round. "What do you want with me?"

Jerry held out a hand. "I want to help you."

Rosie started to leave, and Gunter moved in front of her. Rosie opened her mouth and let out a blood-curdling scream. A baby wailed directly behind him, and Jerry turned toward the commotion and saw a man and woman with two children in tow. The woman pushing a baby stroller knelt to soothe the infant as a boy who looked to be between four and five lifted his arm and pointed in their direction. "Mommy, that man scared Sissy."

Jerry held up his hands and shook his head.

The little boy scrunched up his face and yelled to be heard over his sister's crying. "Not the man with the dog. The one wearing a hat."

Jerry looked at Rosie, who promptly disappeared. All of Jerry's previous bravado disappeared when he saw the look on the mother's face. Not at liberty to leave the scene with such grace, nor wishing to face a mother who looked ready to scratch his eyes out, Jerry motioned for Gunter to follow and hurried off in the opposite direction.

Chapter Ten

There were about thirty cars in the hotel parking lot when Jerry returned, the black sedan among them. He backed into an open space, walked over, and placed a hand on the sedan's hood – cool to the touch. *It's been here for a while.* That the guys even needed a hotel room let him know they were from out of town. *Unless they just want to keep tabs on your comings and goings.*

Jerry went back to the Durango to collect his gun bag and saw his laundry bag sitting on the seat beside it. *Geesh, was that today? It feels like a week ago.*

Jerry picked up both bags and looked at Gunter. "The bed is mine tonight."

Kenny was just stepping around from the back room. He looked up, saw Jerry, and his face turned ashen. *Either he's up to something or has a guilty conscience for taking my money.* Jerry started toward him. Kenny scurried back in the direction he'd just come. *Maybe I should send the dog after him.*

Gunter growled his eagerness. Jerry lowered a

hand to soothe him. "Not yet, Buddy."

The thought of going to bed was enticing, but he'd had a taste for a beer ever since he'd eaten the hotdogs. Jerry was halfway to the hotel bar when he remembered the firepower he was carrying and decided to make a trip to his room to drop off his bags first. As he passed the front desk, Jerry looked for Kenny, but the guy was nowhere in sight. The hair on the back of Jerry's neck prickled. Jerry instantly regretted his decision not to let Gunter go after the guy.

The prickling sensation continued all the way up the stairs and grew stronger as they neared his hotel room. Jerry saw the room number and stood staring at the door, debating. Something told him he was walking into a trap. The fact that Gunter now stood beside him wearing his K-9 vest told him the dog felt it as well. Gunter's ears were forward, his tail held straight as he quivered with anticipation. Someone was on the other side of the door, and from Gunter's alert stance, whoever was in there intended to do him harm. Gunter stuck his head through the door, looked to the right, and emitted a deep growl. Jerry lowered his hand and whispered so as not to be heard. "Easy, boy."

Whoever was in there was most likely standing behind the door since that was the direction the dog's head had turned.

Jerry reached for his key card. Gunter started

barking and growling, spraying saliva all over the carpet and door. Jerry wasn't worried about the noise the dog was making as he felt certain he was the only one that could hear him. If not, the hallway would now be full of pissed-off bystanders complaining about the racket. The fact that the person waiting for him was standing behind the door let him know whoever was waiting for him knew he was coming. *No wonder Kenny was acting so suspicious. I'll deal with him later.*

Jerry set down his bags, pulled his pistol, and tapped the keycard to the computerized lock. The light turned green, and he pulled the lever to open the door. Gunter pushed past him, turned to face the door, and increased his warning. Jerry knew all he had to do was give the command, and Gunter would react. The result would be effective, but he wanted whoever was in his room able to answer questions.

He scanned the room as he pushed open the door, noting the couch, chair, and bed. All as they were when he left the room. What wasn't there this morning was the faint odor of stale cigarettes. Gripping the pistol, he stepped through the doorway and slammed his shoulder into the door. The action was met with a solid thud. The person on the other side of the door was knocked into the back wall as a pistol slid across the floor in front of him.

Jerry kicked the pistol out of reach and then stepped around the door to see a man dressed in a black sweatshirt with the hood pulled over his head. Jerry pointed his gun at the guy as he stooped to retrieve the one on the floor. "What's your name?"

"Bite me!"

"Odd name, but I've heard worse. I think I'll just call you Ballsy, since it was a pretty ballsy move to break into my room with two cops sleeping in the room next door. On your feet, Ballsy. Pull your hood down so I can see your face."

Ballsy had the audacity to extend his hand for Jerry to help him to his feet.

"What are you, high?" Jerry scoffed.

"No, but I wish I was." Ballsy grunted as he rose to his feet. The curtains were closed, the dark room casting shadows over the man, a problem exacerbated by the fact that the man had the hood pulled up on a sweatshirt it was too warm to wear. Jerry tried to look him in the eyes, something impossible with the hood shrouding his face.

Jerry kept the gun leveled at the guy. "I said to pull your hood down. No, keep your right hand where I can see it and use your left."

Ballsy winced as he lifted his arm. To his credit, he didn't mention the pain. Jerry looked him over, and noted his dark, wide-spaced eyes and square chin. His hair was clipped close to his head, and there was something about the way the guy moved that gave Jerry the impression he'd spent time in the service. Under any other circumstances, he would have asked him, but given the guy was hiding in his room, possibly waiting to put a bullet in him, Jerry wasn't much in the mood for swapping stories.

Instead, Jerry pointed the gun at him. "Turn around and assume the position."

Ballsy turned and planted his feet a foot apart and gasped as he raised his arms in the air. Feeling little sympathy, Jerry used his boot to spread the man's legs further. He kept his pistol in his right hand as he used his left to check for any remaining weapons. Not for the first time since quitting his job on the force, Jerry wished for a pair of cuffs to restrain the man.

Jerry glanced at Gunter, then turned the guy and motioned toward the computer chair on the other side of the room. "Sit."

Ballsy lowered his arms and walked to the chair without argument. Once the man was settled, Jerry returned his gun to his waistband. He remembered the bags he'd left in the hall and thought about giving Gunter the command to watch their captive while he retrieved them. No need, as Gunter had yet to stand down. It was easy to see the dog wasn't pleased he had been denied the takedown as he still had on his police vest and currently stood directly in front of Ballsy with his teeth bared.

Jerry smiled at the dog before turning his back on Ballsy to go into the hall to retrieve his bags. As he stepped into the hall, he allowed the door to close behind him. Gathering the bags, he counted to ten before using his keycard to reenter the room. As he entered, he turned on the light.

As expected, Ballsy was lying face down on the floor with Gunter hovering over him. By his position in the middle of the floor, it was obvious the dog had given the man a little lead before taking him down.

Jerry ignored the situation and placed his gun bag in the wardrobe. He sat his ditty bag on the bed before addressing the guy. "I thought I told you to sit on the chair."

Ballsy's eyes were round with fear. "Something pushed me down."

Jerry struggled to keep a blank face. "Before or after you got out of the chair?"

"Huh?"

Jerry took a step closer. When he spoke, he did so as if talking to a child who'd disobeyed a rule. "Did that something knock you down while you were still sitting or after you got up."

"I didn't get up. Something pushed me out of my chair."

Jerry gave a slight nod of the head, and Gunter placed his paws on the middle of the man's back. His eyes bugged even further as he bent his right arm and tried unsuccessfully to bat at his unseen assailant. "Get it off of me."

"Get what off? I don't see anything." *Gunter, if you can hear me, ease up.* Gunter lowered to his haunches, easing the weight off the guy's back.

Jerry squatted where the man could see him. "How'd you get in?" It was a moot question as Jerry already knew the answer. He just wanted to make certain before he turned Gunter loose on the guy.

"The hotel clerk."

"Which one?"

"The guy at the desk. I don't know his name."

"What are you doing in my room?"

"I was robbing you."

Jerry didn't like the answer. He motioned to Gunter, who stood and repositioned, thus adding weight to the guy's left shoulder.

"Ow! How are you doing that?" Ballsy asked as he struggled for relief.

"How doesn't matter. If you want it to stop, you'll answer my questions truthfully."

"I was waiting for you."

"Why?"

"I wanted to talk to you."

"You didn't want anything. Tell me who sent you and why."

Jerry gave the nod, and Gunter pushed off with his front paws, jumping up and landing as the man cried out in pain. Jerry knew it was only a matter of time before they had company.

"Who sent you?"

"He'll kill me if I tell."

Jerry heard voices in the next room. He lowered

his voice and took a chance. "Mario Fabel is the least of your worries."

"If you knew who sent me, why didn't you just say so?"

Jerry ignored the question. "What does Fabel want with me?"

"I don't know."

"He sent you here to kill me."

"Kill you? No. I was supposed to ask you nicely. If that didn't work, I was supposed to rough you up a little. You know, just enough to convince you to meet with him."

The adjoining door clicked open, and Fred hurled himself inside as the spring-loaded door slammed closed behind him. Wearing a t-shirt, black socks, and boxers, the man carried a pistol three times the size of the one Jerry used. If not for the fact that the man's boxers were covered with quarter-sized red hearts, Jerry would have thought him to be a real badass. Before Jerry could tell him he had the situation under control, the door opened once more. Seeming uncharacteristically coolheaded, Barney stepped inside. Wearing pajama pants, he leveled his pistol at Ballsy.

"Help, this guy broke into my room and assaulted me," Ballsy yelled from his position on the floor.

Fred raised an eyebrow at Jerry. "Care to tell me what's going on, or is this some kind of lover's quarrel?"

"Says the man wearing heart boxers." Jerry chuckled. "You mean you don't buy the bit about my breaking into his room?"

Fred shook his head. "Get up."

Ballsy struggled for a moment, then collapsed on the carpet. "I can't."

Fred wrinkled his brow. "Why not?"

"Because someone's standing on my back."

Fred's scowl deepened. He gave a nod to Barney. "Get him up."

Gunter backed away as Barney grabbed Ballsy by the arm and dragged him to his feet.

Jerry handed Fred the man's pistol. "He said his name is Bite Me. Consider him evidence."

Fred unloaded the pistol. "Evidence of what?"

"Evidence that Fabel is in town. Jerk here said Fabel wants to meet with me."

"Did he say when or where?"

Jerry shook his head. "We were just getting to the details when you busted in."

"We'll take him down to the station and get it out of him."

Feeling braver, Ballsy smiled. "I want my lawyer."

Jerry looked at Fred. "Leave him with me."

Fred wavered.

Jerry firmed his voice. "He came to see me, and we are not finished chatting yet."

Ballsy shook his head. “Oh no, you don’t. Take me with you. There’s something weird going on in here.”

“You boys can’t take him to the station dressed like that. Go get dressed. It’ll take you what? Ten minutes? I’ll watch over him and keep him safe until you come back to get him. Just to show you I’m playing by the rules, you can take this.” Jerry pulled his pistol from his waistband and handed it to Fred.

Fred sighed. “You say he came into your room to have a chat?”

“That’s what he told me.”

“You think ten minutes will be enough time to finish your conversation?”

“It will, and I give you my word I won’t lay a hand on the man.”

Ballsy started for the adjoining door. “I demand you take me with you.”

Fred glared at the man. “Take one more step, and I’ll shoot you myself and tell the cops you were trying to make a break for it.”

Ballsy gulped. “I thought you were the cops.”

Fred reached for the doorknob. “I never said that. McNeal, did you ever hear me say I was a cop?”

Jerry smiled and shook his head. “Nope. As a matter of fact, you made it perfectly clear you weren’t one.”

Chapter Eleven

Jerry sat in the hotel bar sipping a bottle of ice-cold Bud. Gunter lay next to him in the seat with his head resting in Jerry's lap. It had been a long day for them both. While Jerry was looking forward to taking a shower and going to bed, he'd promised to meet with his new friends after they passed Ballsy over to the patrolmen who were on their way to collect him. The meeting was of Jerry's doing, as while Ballsy had been very forthcoming with information once left in the room with Jerry and Gunter, Jerry had not been as open when passing the guy off to the men in the next room.

Fred and Barney entered the room. Jerry raised his bottle to get their attention. Fred elbowed Barney, and the two men started in his direction. Fred sat in the seat on the opposite side. Barney slid in next to him. The waitress followed them over, and both men ordered Bud Light on tap.

Jerry waited for the waitress to leave before speaking. "Nice of you two to join me."

Fred stifled a yawn. "Didn't see as we had much choice in the matter."

Jerry grinned. "What can I say? I was tired of drinking alone." Gunter lifted his head and grumbled his displeasure. Jerry scratched the dog behind the ear to soothe him.

Barney snickered and elbowed Fred, who nearly choked on his beer. Fred lowered his glass. "Can't you wait until you get back to your room before doing that?"

Jerry looked down at his lap, then back at the two men. "I'm scratching my dog."

Barney broke into an uncontrolled laugh.

Fred's face remained serious. "I don't care what it's called. Stop doing it."

Jerry blew out a sigh. "I'm not playing with myself. Gunter is here, and I'm scratching him behind the ear."

The laughter stopped. Both men scooched forward, looking over the table to get a better view. Jerry raised an eyebrow. "Now who looks like the perverts?"

Fred dropped back in his seat, but Barney was slower to respond. He nodded toward Jerry's lap. "You're telling me there's a dog in your lap, right this minute."

"No, just his head."

Barney's eyes bugged. Jerry realized the man misinterpreted what he'd said. "It's a German shepherd. They are big dogs. He's lying across the seat with his head in my lap."

Barney relaxed. "Oh. You had me for a moment. I wasn't sure how this whole ghost thing worked."

Fred held up a hand. "Before we get into all that, I want to know what you learned from our friend in the room."

Jerry eyed the two sitting across from him. "Me first. I ponied up to things on my end earlier, and you left without telling me who you worked for."

Fred smiled. "Another mistake on your part. You got distracted and didn't push the issue."

Jerry slammed his fist on the table. Gunter was on instant alert. "I'm tired of these cat and mouse games." Jerry ran a hand down the length of the dog's back. "Easy, fellow."

Fred swallowed and took a gulp of beer. Barney looked somewhat ready to call it a night. Seeing he had their attention, Jerry played his advantage. "Tell me what you want, or my friend here will help me interrogate you."

Fred lowered his glass. "That sounded a bit like a threat."

Jerry didn't want trouble. He merely wanted answers. "I just want the truth."

Fred sat back in his seat. He touched Barney's arm, and the man relaxed. "Okay, McNeal, what is it you want to know?"

"For starters, I want to know your real names."

"Easy. You've got them."

"You're telling me Fred and Barney are your real

names and you two just happen to be partners?"

Fred poked a thumb toward his chest. "As you already know, my name is Alfred Jefferies. This here is Barnaby Hendershot. We both used to go by our first names until we were teamed together about eight years ago. Some meandering wiseass who didn't even work in our unit came in for training, offhandedly referred to us as Fred and Barney, and it stuck."

Instead of being let down, Jerry was glad to find out their names were real. Real enough anyway. He'd gotten used to the pseudonyms, sometimes had trouble remembering names, and didn't want to have to go through the trouble of forgetting what he knew. "Okay, so now for the really hard question. Who exactly do you two work for?"

Fred seemed to be the answer man. Barney appeared ready to let him do the talking. "The government."

Jerry chuckled. "That's a pretty broad answer."

"I'm afraid it's all I'm prepared to give at the moment. You come to work for us, I'll read you in on everything you need to know."

Jerry had been in mid-sip and glanced at Fred over his beer bottle. "Is that a job offer?"

Fred smiled. "Do you want it to be?"

Jerry finished his beer and signaled the waitress for another round. "I'm not looking for a job."

"Just because you don't need the money doesn't

mean you don't need the benefits our agency can offer."

"I already have health insurance."

"I'm not talking about those kind of benefits." Fred grew quiet as the waitress approached with new drinks and collected the empties. After she'd gone, he continued. "Our agency has a different kind of insurance."

"Such as?"

"Such as not having to lie about being a cop."

"No, I'd just have to lie about who I work for."

"You'd have a legitimate cover and documentation to back it up. Credentials that would open any door without question." Jerry started to remind the man that he himself had never bothered to show Jerry any such documentation when Fred started talking again. "And the biggest draw, if you ask me, is it would keep your old pal Seltzer out of hot water. He puts his can in a sling every time he covers for you."

And that was the catalyst that made Jerry even consider the man's proposal. Still, he'd walked away from enough jobs that he decided to mull this one over a bit more before asking for further details. "Mark Ruggles."

Fred cocked his head as if he hadn't heard. "Who's that?"

"The name of the guy that was in my room."

"A far cry from Ballsy."

"Even further from Bite Me. He works for Fabel and claims he was only there to talk."

"And the gun?"

"In case I wasn't interested in having a conversation."

"Did he tell you what he wanted to talk about?"

"Yep, he said Fabel wants to meet with me."

"About?"

"He didn't say."

"Didn't say or didn't know?"

"Said he didn't know. Said Fabel wants to meet me tomorrow morning at ten. Said the guy would be alone and unarmed."

"And you believed him?"

"He was telling the truth."

"That's a pretty big gamble if you decide to go."

"I'm going, and not a gamble. Like I said, the guy was telling the truth."

"How can you be so sure?"

Jerry leaned back, stretched, then rested his arms on the back of the booth. "Imagine you are standing there getting interrogated. Every time you answer a question incorrectly, something squeezes your junk. Now, to make things interesting, the person who is asking the questions is halfway across the room."

"Sounds like a cool party trick."

"No trick. At least not on my part. Just a ninety-pound ghost who takes great pleasure in sniffing crotches."

"Is that dog with you all the time?"

Jerry nodded.

"Did I mention the job comes with a company car of your choosing?"

Jerry ignored the comment. "How'd you know about the dog?"

"I didn't. Not for certain anyway – until you confirmed it."

"You looked right at him."

"Not until after you did. I just followed your gaze."

Jerry sighed and closed his eyes. *Way to go, McNeal.*

"Don't beat yourself up. You're good. Real good. But, when it comes to your abilities, you have a weakness. I've seen it before, which is why I know you have the potential to be even better. That's what training is for."

"You said you've seen it before. Are you saying your agency goes around hiring people with special powers?"

Both men laughed a genuine laugh. It was Fred who answered. "Not in the way your mind just led you to believe. This is not a children's television show. It is real life. Unless you can fly, disappear, or any other of the superhero things you see on television, the answer is no. Our agency seeks out real people with real skills that can help us do our jobs."

That his answer was as vague as the job offer he'd proposed was not lost on Jerry. "So tell me, Alfred, what is your superpower?"

Fred grinned. "They hired me for my charming disposition."

Jerry resisted the urge to roll his eyes. He looked at Barney, who'd been conspicuously quiet. "And yours?"

"That I don't complain about sharing a room with a man who insists on wearing boxers with tiny hearts on them." Barney cast a glance at Fred and winked.

Fred chuckled. "The wife bought them for me."

Jerry glanced at Fred's hand. There was no sign of the man ever having worn a ring.

"We don't wear them."

For a moment, Jerry thought the man had read his mind, then realized the guy had merely seen him looking at his hand and guessed his thoughts.

"Our line of work dictates we use a certain level of caution to see our loved ones safe. You, for one, should understand the reason."

Instantly, Jerry thought of Seltzer and his wife June.

"Take your friend Seltzer for instance." Fred smiled when Jerry's head snapped up. "In some ways, you are very predictable, Mr. McNeal. Take this hotel, for instance. While we had some things in place on the off chance you surprised us, we felt you would choose this one."

Once again, Jerry eyed the man over his beer. "You stayed at one in New York. You are a creature of habit. It stands to reason you would choose this hotel. It feels safe to you."

Wrong. I chose this because it reminded me of Holly.

"Then again, you may have chosen it because it reminded you of that woman from the accident in Pennsylvania," Barney interjected.

Jerry stiffened, and Gunter poked his head up, growling at the men. Jerry ran his hand over his head. "You said you weren't sure about Gunter. But obviously, you knew something, or you wouldn't have asked."

The bar lights flickered.

Jerry couldn't help noticing the look of relief that crossed Fred's face. *What is he hiding?* Maybe nothing, but the guy obviously wasn't ready to spill all his secrets. Jerry reached for his wallet. "Looks like we'll have to continue this conversation."

Fred looked at his watch and slid a card onto the table just as the waitress approached. He winked at Jerry as she walked away. "It's on my boss."

Jerry motioned Gunter down and slid out of the booth. Kenny was behind the counter as the trio made their way to the elevator. Jerry started to beg off the elevator ride, wanting to have a chat with the guy.

Fred crooked a finger and drew him closer. "Don't worry about your friend Seltzer or his wife. We've had someone on both of them ever since we learned of Fabel's threat."

Jerry rocked back on his heels. "Why would you care about them?"

Fred shook his head. "We don't. It's you we're interested in. And because we are, we've put certain structures in place to keep those close to you safe. That includes your parents."

Jerry wanted to be angry that an agency he knew nothing about was keeping tabs on his family. But the truth of the matter was he hadn't considered Fabel going after them. "My parents?"

Barney bobbed his head. "From what I hear, your mom's a hoot."

Fred stepped into the elevator and held the door. "You won't be very good to us if you are mourning your family and friends. Are you coming?"

Jerry shook his head. "I've got some unfinished business with my friend behind the counter."

"Don't kill him. The agency frowns upon unsanctioned killings."

Jerry frowned. "As opposed to sanctioned killings?"

Fred shrugged and let go of the door.

Jerry pivoted. As he did, an image of Holly came to mind. Fred said there were structures in place to watch over those he cared about. Did that include

Holly and her daughter? Jerry turned to ask, sighing as the elevator door slid closed.

***

Jerry positioned himself where he could see the front desk without being seen in return and had spent the last ten minutes leaning against the wall waiting for the drunk at the counter to finish his political rant. That the guy was even able to recall who the president was in his highly intoxicated state was impressive. More impressive was Kenny's ability to listen without offering commentary. So impressed was Jerry that he was currently considering pushing off his place against the wall and heading to bed.

Gunter barked.

Jerry chuckled and kneeled to where the dog could hear him. "I know I said you can take care of him. It was just a thought. I'm not going to break my promise."

The telephone rang and Kenny answered. Not having an audience, Mr. Intoxicated sauntered off down the hall. Jerry waited for Kenny to end the call before approaching the desk.

Kenny looked up and all color drained from his face. He started to leave. Jerry shook his head. "Not so fast, son. We have some unfinished business to tend to."

Kenny gulped and looked side to side, but stayed rooted in place.

Jerry leaned over the counter. "Playing both

sides of the field is going to get you hurt."

Another gulp. "What do you mean?"

So much for being smart. "What did Alfred offer you to get you to put me in the room next to him?"

"I have some speeding tickets. He said he would make them go away."

Okay, fair deal. "What about the guy today?"

Kenny blinked his confusion. "What guy today?"

Gunter growled. Jerry showed him his palm to silence him. He lowered his voice. "Don't play with me, son."

When Kenny spoke, his voice trembled. "I'm not fooling around. I don't know what guy you're talking about."

Jerry knew the boy was telling the truth. But it didn't make sense. "A guy came into my room a few hours ago and tried to kill me. According to him, you gave him the key."

Kenny's eyes widened. "The dude the police took out of here?"

Jerry nodded. "That's the one."

Kenny threw his hands up and splayed his hands. "No, no, no. I didn't do that on purpose. He came to the counter when I was checking someone in. He seemed to be in a hurry. I mean, he wouldn't even wait for me to finish with the couple I was checking in. He handed me his room key and told me it didn't work. I asked him what room and he told me. That was it."

"Do you remember what room?"

"Sure, room 207."

Jerry pulled the folder with his room key from his pocket. "What number does this say?"

Beads of sweat appeared at Kenny's temple. He shook his head. "Honest, Mister, I didn't know. I was just trying to get the guy to move on so he didn't upset the couple at the counter."

Jerry looked at Gunter and the dog licked his lips. Jerry wagged his finger. "Sorry, boy. You can't eat him, but you can sniff his balls."

Kenny kept his hands up but stretched his neck as if looking for who Jerry was talking to, then knitted his brows and looked at Jerry.

Gunter slinked around the counter and took great delight in sniffing the guy's crotch. As Kenny backed away from the unseen invasion of his personal space, Jerry smiled and left without another word.

Chapter Twelve

Jerry parked within sight of the *Friendship* and looked for any sign of Fabel or the black Lincoln he'd seen the previous day. Not seeing either, he got out. Gunter stayed at his side as they made their way toward the ship. Jerry stopped about a hundred feet from the two-story wooden structure that looked like it had been there for over a hundred years. Just off center in the south window of the front of the building was a yellow and white banner with an owl. The word "owl" was written in teal on the bottom left corner, with no other information given about the significance of the banner.

Jerry stepped to the right of the building, looked up, and saw a white sign that read Sail Loft. The hairs on the back of his neck tingled. The feeling was gone when he walked to the back of the building. Jerry retraced his steps and once again felt the tingle. He looked at Gunter. "Do you feel that?"

Gunter wagged his tail.

Jerry circled the building twice before deciding to have a peek inside. He walked up the ramp and tried the door, only to find it locked. There were windows on the first floor, but the building was lifted with brick stilts, and Jerry wasn't tall enough to see inside. As he turned, he saw a face peering out. Not able to see due to the glare of the sun, Jerry stepped forward for a closer look. Though he'd only seen the woman for a moment the evening prior, he'd seen enough of her to know the face in the window belonged to Rosie Freeman.

He stared into the window. *Come out so we can talk.*

A gunshot sounded in the distance. Jerry whirled, only relaxing when he realized the sound he'd heard was the backfire from a passing car. When he looked back toward the window, Rosie was gone.

His cell rang, alerting him to a call. Jerry looked at the screen. *Unknown.*

Gunter placed his nose to the ground, caught a whiff of something only he could smell, and raced across the lawn. Jerry swiped to answer the call.

"It's not too late to put on a wire, you know."

Jerry sighed heavily into the phone.

"You sound disgusted."

Jerry ran his hand over his head. "You could say that."

"You can't let the job get to you."

"What job? I can't even do what I came here for because I'm too busy trying to stay alive. There's a murderer on the loose, and I'm standing here waiting for someone who may not show."

"He'll show."

"You know something you're not telling me."

"I just got word Fabel was spotted heading this way. Looks to be about five minutes out."

"So much for the wire."

"You don't like wires, remember?"

"I don't like getting dead either."

"Don't you worry about that. Just stay in the open. Whatever you do, don't put yourself between Fabel and the street."

"Dare I ask why?"

Fred chuckled. "You were a Marine. Figure it out."

Jerry didn't have to figure it out. He already knew. A sniper's gun couldn't hit what it couldn't see. Jerry took in a breath. "Is Fabel a sanctioned kill?"

"Only if he tries to take you out."

"Good to know." Jerry saw the Lincoln pull to the curb and slipped his phone into his breast pocket. The moment Fabel exited the SUV, Gunter was at Jerry's side. Wearing his police K-9 vest, the dog was ready for action. His ears tilted forward, watching the man as he approached. Jerry cut across the yard. Fabel matched his move, cutting to the center of the field. Jerry kept his back to the water and Fabel seemed comfortable facing him.

Fabel lifted his arms and splayed his fingers. "I'm unarmed. Want to frisk me?"

"No need. I hear you are a man of your word." Actually, Jerry didn't trust the man as far as he could throw him, but between the sniper and the fact that Gunter was highly focused on the man's every move, Jerry felt the situation to be under control.

Fabel lowered his arms but kept his hands away from his body. "I heard you were coming to town. Gutsy move since you had to have known I'd be wanting to finish our chat. So I thought to myself, Jerry's a smart guy. What would make him risk his life to come here? Not sightseeing. I have it on good authority you don't take time to actually see any of the places you visit."

Jerry started to ask him if he'd been chatting with his grandmother but felt the man wouldn't see the humor in the question.

"So I had my guys do some digging. What do you think they found?"

Jerry took a chance. "A missing redhead?"

Fabel snapped the fingers of his right hand. "Bingo. So back to my original thought that maybe you were in on this and traveling around finding the bodies to collect the reward. Only you know what else I found out?"

"That there wasn't a reward on finding Rosie Freeman?" Not because the family didn't have money, but because Rosie had been a troubled teen who had run away more times than the family could count. While her disappearance had raised suspicion within the community and among her peers, as far as her family was concerned, Rosie had merely tired of college and found an ingenious way of ditching her student loans.

"Precisely. So that got me to thinking about your story and, to put it simply, I believe you."

"Lucky me."

"Indeed. Because if I didn't, I would have my men kill that sniper of yours and put a bullet in your skull as well."

Gunter growled.

Easy, boy. Gunter eased his stance but stayed focused on the man in front of him. "So, you know I'm not involved with their murders. Then why are you here?"

"Because I think we are on the same team."

"Not even close."

"Okay. But we want the same thing."

Jerry rocked back on his heels. "Which is?"

"We want to see whoever is doing this castrated."

Jerry gave a slight shrug. "I'm not sure they do that in prison, but I'm sure with your connections, it can be arranged."

"No, here's the thing. The man's not going to prison."

"He's not?"

"No. That's why I'm here."

Jerry smiled. "Let me guess. You're going to

make me an offer I can't refuse."

Fabel bobbed his head. "See, I knew you were a smart man."

"Smart enough not to get into bed with you."

Fabel's jaw twitched. "I'm offering you the deal of a lifetime. Hear me out. You find this dirtbag. You hand him over to me. In turn, you find a little something extra in your stocking on Christmas Day."

"What if I don't believe in Santa?"

Fabel frowned. "Of course you believe in Santa. Everyone should. I know him personally. He's a jolly guy. You've seen the red suit. How could anyone wear something that dope and not be jolly? I have a card. Can I give it to you?"

"No need. I've got your number."

"Still. I want you to have it just to make sure." Fabel reached into his breast pocket with two fingers and pulled out a business card, handing it to Jerry.

Jerry looked the card over but didn't see anything out of the ordinary.

Fabel turned. "See those houses over there? They have a million-dollar view. Some of them even have a two-million-dollar view. You could see yourself living in one of those, couldn't you?"

"I'm not taking your bribe, Fabel."

"I'm not offering you a bribe. I want you to bring him to me out of the goodness of your heart. In the name of justice and all. In return, the man handing out the presents will be informed that little Jerry's been extra good this year."

"You sound like a creepy pedophile."

Fabel's face lost all humor. "I sound like a man who wants to see justice done."

"That's why I will do this by the book. I will track him down and make sure there is enough evidence to make the case stick."

"He'll walk. All your witnesses are dead."

"If he walks, he's all yours. I'll even help you find him. Until then, we do this my way. And my way is to see him in front of that judge."

Fable narrowed his eyes. "For what purpose?"

"Because I want the prosecutor to read off all his crimes and list each victim's name so he will know them for who they were and not a hash mark carved into his chest like a prize for a job well done." Jerry realized he was shaking and took in a long breath to settle himself.

"He marks himself when he kills?"

Jerry nodded his head.

"I've got people on the inside. Why didn't I know about that?"

"Because the cops didn't know until I told them."

"How do you know?"

"Because Ashley told me so."

Fabel's head snapped up. "You spoke to Ash?"

"I did."

"When?"

"A couple of weeks ago." Jerry could see the emotions washing across the man's face as he grappled with what he'd just heard. Jerry softened his tone. "You asked me how I knew where to find your sister's body. It's because she led me to it."

"You're saying you can talk to the dead."

"Some of them."

"And you spoke to my sister after she died?"

"Yes."

"How was she? Is she okay?"

"Her spirit remembered what happened to her. She was confused at first, but Max and I were able to help her. Finding her body gave her peace. But what she really wants is justice. Just not in the way you're suggesting."

"How can you be so sure?"

"Because she told me so. She told me her family was connected. She said her brother was overprotective. That was the reason she took off without telling you she was going."

"Ash blames me for her death?"

"No. She blames herself. She's had plenty of time to Monday morning quarterback."

"I'm her brother. We're family. She needs to let me put it right." As Fabel spoke, he paced in a circle. While Jerry stood back, Gunter was at the ready, matching his every move.

"No. If you kill him, that will only make you feel better. She knows there were other victims and wants them and their families to see the man put to trial. That way, everyone can get the closure they need."

"If I let him go to trial, can I take care of him in prison?"

Jerry shrugged. "The federal prison is out of my jurisdiction."

Fabel rolled his neck. "And you're not just telling me this to get me off your back."

"I don't take my gift lightly."

Fabel shook his head. "No, I don't guess you would. Alright then. We have a deal."

Jerry started to hand the man his card back.

Fabel shook his head. "Keep it. I have friends in some very high places. If you need anything – a private jet to get you somewhere, cash to see this through – name it. It's not a bribe. It's funding to see this man caught and see that justice is done."

Jerry pocketed the card.

Fabel turned to leave and hesitated. "Is she here?"

"Ashley?"

Fabel nodded.

"No."

"But you think she'll be in the courtroom?"

Jerry nodded his head. "I'd place money on it."

"Good." With that, Fabel turned. He took several steps then returned. "I'll tell my men to stand down. No harm will come to anyone you know on account of me."

Jerry answered with a nod. Fabel turned once more. This time, he didn't look back.

Jerry waited until Fabel was out of earshot before pulling his phone from his front pocket. "Did you get all that?"

"Smart move leaving your cell on."

"I'm a smart man."

"You took a chance telling him your secrets."

"I didn't tell him something he didn't already know."

"How can you be so sure?"

"Trust me. I can tell."

"You coming back to the hotel?"

Jerry looked toward the man in the striped shirt and white pants who'd showed up just as Fabel arrived and had witnessed the whole conversation. "No, I'll be along in a bit. I have a few things to take care of first."

Chapter Thirteen

It was difficult to keep from laughing watching the unearthly man hop around like a schoolgirl playing hopscotch. Both hands centered across his groin area, the man wasn't at all pleased by Gunter's inquisitive greeting.

"My name is Cornelius Pattengill. I beg you to call off your mutt."

He's not a mutt. He's a pure breed German shepherd – not to mention a highly trained police dog. Jerry kept that thought to himself, as he didn't think Mr. Pattengill would be the least bit impressed with Gunter's pedigree. Especially since the dog was determined to get up close and personal with the fellow's man parts. "Gunter, leave it."

Gunter ignored the command.

"Gunter, cease!"

Once again, the dog ignored Jerry's order.

"Gunter, leave that guy's junk alone!"

Gunter withdrew his muzzle, looked at Jerry, and yawned.

"Good boy. Now get over here."

The overzealous canine lowered his tail and

made his way to Jerry looking much like a dog who'd lost his favorite ball. Jerry snickered. In a way, that was precisely the case. Jerry turned his attention to the apparition. "Is there something I can do for you, sir?"

The spirit eyed Gunter. "You are he, are you not?"

Jerry lifted a brow. "He who?"

"Him. The man who can speak to spirits." Cornelius chuckled. "Of course, you are he, or we would not be having this conversation. Then again, I seem to be doing all the talking. But you must be him. You simply must."

Gunter stretched his head and took a step forward.

"Gunter. No. Mr. Pattengill, how can I help you?"

The lines in the spirit's face crinkled, then he blew out a long sigh. "It's about the girl."

Jerry sucked in a breath. "Which girl?"

"Well, the one you came to find, of course. It's all over town. How you came to find her, but I'm here to tell you that you have a problem."

Besides the fact spirits are talking about me? Jerry ran his hand over his head. "What is my problem?"

"Well, I guess it is not your problem exactly, but more to do with the girl. You see, she doesn't know she's dead. I know she is, and the rest of us in town know she is, but she flitters about like she owns the whole city. We all have our stations, and does she abide by the rules? No! Mrs. Reynolds caught her in the gift shop. The gift shop! Mrs. Reynolds has been haunting that store for decades. I'm telling you, it just isn't done." Cornelius nodded toward the *Friendship*. "Why, I've even caught her on my ship a time or two."

Jerry looked at the tall, masted sailing ship tied to the pier. "Your ship?"

"Why, I'm the harbor master, am I not? That means everything along the waterfront is under my supervision. As such, it is my duty to see that things are as they should be. That ship is no place for a lady. Not that she's acting like one."

"They give tours of the ship. Surely, you've seen other women come aboard?" Why he was even discussing the matter, Jerry hadn't a clue.

"Of course, they allow women on board – if they are accompanied. We have rules, I'm telling you. A person buys a ticket, and the tour guide takes them through the ship. Occasionally, a person goes it alone, but always someone lets them in and knows they are on board. But not this one. No, she just appears out of nowhere. I'm telling you, it just isn't proper."

Jerry did his best to appear sympathetic. "Do you know where Ms. Freeman is at this very moment?"

"Well, no. But I'd expect it is someplace she

doesn't belong."

Jerry tried not to buy in to the whole turf war thing, but curiosity got the better of him. "People die all the time. So, if every place in town is already spoken for, what is a spirit to do?"

Cornelius frowned. "They apply for a secondary spot, of course."

"This application. Is it like a job application?"

"Boy, they have you pegged wrong," Cornelius huffed. "They made it sound as if you were all-knowing."

Jerry suddenly wondered who the "they" were the man kept referring to. He shook his head. "Nope, just learning as I go."

Gunter lowered to the ground and gathered his legs under his body, attempting to crawl closer to the man. Cornelius didn't seem to notice, so Jerry kept quiet.

"Okay, here's how it works." Before the man could utter another word, the skin on the back of Jerry's neck tingled. Gunter snapped his head around. Springing to his feet, he yipped in the direction of the ancient building.

Jerry looked up to see Rosie peering out a second-story window.

Cornelius tapped him on the shoulder. "There she is. Get her!"

"What do you mean, get her? I'm not a ghostbuster."

"A what?"

"I don't capture spirits."

"Then what good are you?"

I have no idea. "Listen, are you able to get me inside the building?"

"Well, if that don't beat all. You can't even walk through walls."

Jerry had the sudden urge to toss the man in the water.

Cornelius must have picked up on it as he took a step back. "Okay. I'll pop inside and undo the lock, but after that, you're on your own."

"Works for me." Cornelius disappeared, and Jerry hurried toward the building. The door was unlocked. Jerry pushed it open to see Gunter waiting inside. The dog smiled a K-9 smile and greeted him with a wag of the tail. Jerry gave him a quick pat to let him know he was glad for the company. The windows on the first floor were uncovered. There was enough light to see the area was devoid of ghosts. Jerry looked toward the stairs. "Let's find Rosie, boy. Easy. Remember, we don't want to scare her."

Gunter lowered his nose to the ground and raced up the dark staircase. Jerry wasted no time following after the dog. He topped the stairs and saw them. Rosie Freeman sat cross-legged on the floor with Gunter wiggling, crouched in front of her, covering her face with eager kisses.

Rosie looked up, fading in and out.

Jerry raised his hands in front of him and slowed his approach. "It's alright, Rosie. I'm not here to hurt you."

Rosie's eyes grew wide. "How do you know my name?"

Think, McNeal. "Cornelius told me."

Rosie faded and reappeared. "Whatever he said to you are lies."

"He told me you don't know you are dead." Jerry debated his next sentence. "You've been dead for over three years."

Rosie disappeared.

Jerry sighed. *Way to go, McNeal*. Gunter whined and sidled up against him. Jerry lowered his hand to the dog. "Looks like I blew it."

Gunter led the way down the stairs. Cornelius was nowhere in sight, so Jerry locked the door behind him when he exited the building. He'd nearly reached his SUV when his skin began to crawl. A second later, Cornelius appeared beside him. The vibration surrounding him told Jerry the spirit was upset. Just as Jerry opened his mouth to apologize for fumbling the situation, Cornelius spoke.

"You better get over to Witch City Mall. Your friend is causing quite the to-do. She's already lowered the temperature in the place twenty degrees, and people are leaving in droves. Something like that is bad for tourist season."

Jerry couldn't resist. "You care about tourist season?"

"Of course I do. We spirits here in Salem take pride in giving the tourists a proper welcome. A good scare here and there is good for the town's economy." His face grew serious. "But not this. This here can be bad for us ghosts."

Don't do it, McNeal. "Why's that?"

"The last thing we want is for them to call in someone who really knows what they are doing. Last time that happened, they ran several of us out of town. Myself included, but I came back when things settled down." Cornelius lifted his eyes to the sky. "Oh, she's really causing a stir now."

Jerry started to ask what was happening, but the man disappeared.

***

Unable to find a parking place close to the mall, Jerry parked his Durango a couple streets over and all but ran the short distance to the mall. Jerry estimated the crowd that milled about the entrance to Witch City Mall to be around fifty. Seventy-five if you counted those no longer among the living. Several of the latter gathered together, pointing in his direction and speaking in hushed tones. Gunter barked at the gathering and dove into their fray. The spirits disappeared, and Gunter trotted back to Jerry's side, tongue hanging from his mouth, looking rather pleased with himself.

As Jerry started inside, a mall cop took hold of his elbow, stopping him. "Don't go in there, Buddy. There are some strange happenings. Not to mention the air is stuck on high. It's freezing."

Jerry glanced at the man's hand and looked at him with narrowed eyes. Gunter growled. Jerry gave the dog the signal to stand down.

Taking the warning, the mall cop released him and stepped aside. "Okay, your funeral."

Jerry entered the building. Sure enough, the temperature dropped at least fifty degrees. Jerry's skin crawled, leaving no doubt that Rosie was the root of the problem. He opened his mouth to tell Gunter to stay close, and saw his breath, something that hadn't happened since leaving Pennsylvania. Jerry looked at Gunter. "Seems Ms. Freeman isn't very happy."

Gunter growled a low rumble.

Jerry smiled. "I'm glad one of us feels confident. Lead the way, my friend."

They found her in the photography store trying on witches' hats. She looked up when they entered and plucked a red sequined pointed hat from the rack, trying it on for size. She looked in the mirror, frowned, and tossed it aside.

Jerry looked for the owner of the studio but didn't see anyone. "Are you the only one here?"

Rosie shrugged. "I guess so. I tried to ask the woman to take my picture. She clutched her purse and ran away. I guess she thought I was a thief or something. It happens all the time. I guess they have a thing against redheads."

"No. They have a thing against ghosts."

"They should. The town's full of them." She looked around as if to see if anyone was listening. "I know. I've seen them."

"Have you always been able to see ghosts?"

Rosie scrunched up her face, placed her index finger above her eyebrow, then removed it, pointing it at him. "That's a resounding no."

"Doesn't that tell you anything?"

"Yeah. That this place is mega haunted."

Jerry blew out a sigh – his breath billowing into the room.

Rosie blew out her breath, wrinkling her nose when nothing happened. She knitted her brows together and tried a second time. "Where's my breath?"

"You don't have any."

"Of course I do. If I didn't, I'd be…"

Jerry finished the sentence for her. "Dead."

Rosie pinched her arm. "It doesn't hurt."

Jerry looked at the scissors on the counter. She followed his gaze. "Go ahead, give it a shot."

"Don't tell me again, or I'll do it for real."

"Try it. They won't hurt you."

Rosie tossed the hat aside and walked to the counter. "I'm going to do it."

Jerry shrugged.

She picked up the scissors, jabbed them into her chest, and stood there staring at them protruding from her chest. "Awesome!"

Jerry wasn't sure what he expected from her, but being happy about being dead wasn't it. "You're not upset?"

She pulled the scissors free. "More like relieved. I've been pretty freaked out. I thought maybe someone slipped something in my drink and that I've been on a bad acid trip. One minute, I'm stepping out of my room to have a cigarette. The next, I'm walking around town, seeing all these ghosts. Ghosts are some pretty creepy dudes. I mean, they are like, get out of my house and stay off my ship. One even tried to kick me out of church. I mean, come on, it's a church. They let everyone in."

"Rosie, it's freezing in here. Can you turn off the cooler?"

Rosie's jaw dropped open. "Dude! Are you saying I did that?"

"That's my understanding. Don't you remember?"

"I bumped into this woman and she kind of freaked out, so I told her to chill." A wide smile crossed her face. "Let's heat this place up a bit."

Jerry wagged a finger at her. "Okay, but no fires."

"Party pooper." She shrugged. "You know, I was

beginning not to like this place, but now that I know I'm dead. I think I'll stay."

"I think you'll need to talk to some of the locals before making that decision. Seems they aren't too happy with you."

"Locals. You mean the ghosts?"

"Ghosts, spirits, apparitions. Whatever you feel comfortable with. They are upset you aren't following the rules."

Rosie threw her hands in the air. "Just my luck. Even death has rules."

Gunter barked. Jerry looked to see customers filtering back into the building. "I think we'd better go someplace where we can talk."

"Okay."

Jerry pointed to the hats strewed across the floor. "After you clean up your mess."

"Fine." Rosie gathered the hats and placed them back where she'd found them, and started toward the main entrance. Jerry and Gunter followed. Rosie slowed until they were all walking side by side.

Jerry pulled the Bluetooth from his pocket and slipped it over his ear. "Do you remember anything about the night you died?"

Rosie's energy turned serious. "Maybe. I've had some flashes. But like I said, I just thought I was on one heck of a trip."

They kept walking, meandering in and around people as they strolled the streets, Jerry strategically leading the way to his Durango. He waited until no one could hear before continuing. "I think I know some of the details. But I need you to tell me what you know first. Just to be sure."

"I came here with some friends. It wasn't much of a drive, but we just wanted a break before fall classes started. We'd spent the day doing tourist stuff and had planned on going out clubbing later. I wanted a smoke. Our building didn't allow it, so I went outside."

"Then what happened?"

"Someone put something over my nose. When I woke up, I had a headache and was in the back of a van."

"What color was the van?"

"White. Without windows." Her hand went to her throat. When she removed it, Jerry could see the fingerprints. It had been the same with the others when they stopped to recall their stories. "I tried to get away, but my hands were tied. Not that it mattered. He was stronger than me."

"He raped you?"

She nodded.

"Can you remember anything else?" Jerry knew it was the same man, but he had to hear it from her.

Her eyes misted. "He stopped in the middle of what he was doing and pulled out a knife. I thought he was going to cut me, so I screamed and turned my face away. He grabbed my chin and turned me so I could see, but instead of cutting me, he cut himself. Right here."

Jerry watched as she pointed to the same area the others had mentioned, proving she too had been murdered by the Hash Mark Killer. "Did he say anything else? Tell you his name?"

She wiped at her tears. "No name. He said I was now a part of him. Just like the others. I don't feel like talking anymore. Is that enough?"

Jerry smiled. "Almost. I just need you to show me where your body is buried."

She shook her head. "I couldn't see where he took me. It was dark. And that bell music he was playing was so loud."

Jerry wasn't worried. He knew once they were heading in the right direction, Rosie's spirit would be able to lead them to her earthly body. "I promise you I'm going to find this guy. But we must locate your body so we can give your family some closure."

"I told you I don't know where he took me."

Jerry opened the door to the Durango. Gunter jumped inside and moved to the rear seat. Jerry motioned her inside. "Your spirit does."

Rosie started to get inside and hesitated. "The last time I got in with someone I didn't know, it didn't turn out so well."

Jerry managed a smile. "No one can ever hurt you again, Rosie."

Rosie hoisted herself into the cab, started to close the door, and paused. "On the plus side, I haven't had a cigarette in months. To be honest, I just thought I'd quit cold turkey and was going to rub it in my mom's face the next time she saw me. You know, she used to tell me smoking would kill me. I guess she was right."

Chapter Fourteen

Jerry stepped off the elevator and stopped at room 205, knocking on the door. He was about to knock a second time when the door opened. Fred moved to the side and motioned him in. Jerry looked about the room. It was a mirror image of the one he was in, except there were two queen beds.

Fred saw where his gaze landed and smiled. "I told you I'm a happily married man."

"Good to know."

"Barney's still out at the cemetery overseeing the extraction."

Jerry shuddered at the casualness of the wording. "You guys didn't waste any time."

"We had the judge on standby. Once we got the location, it was just a matter of formalities."

"It must be nice having that kind of pull."

"It is. And having that kind of power at your fingertips intrigues you. I can tell."

"It does, but probably not for the reasons you think."

"Then why?"

"Because every job I've ever had has had rules

in place that keep me from doing what I do."

"And what is it you do?"

"I save people that others can't."

Fred headed to the sofa and motioned Jerry to the easy chair. Gunter didn't wait for an invitation. He jumped onto the nearest bed, pawed at the bedding, and made several circles before lowering and lying with his head on the pillow.

Fred waited until Jerry was seated before continuing. "That is why this position is perfect for you."

Jerry remembered what Rosie had said. *Even death has rules.* "Are you trying to tell me there aren't any rules?"

"None that will prevent you from doing your job."

Something still didn't feel right. "How'd you know about Gunter?"

"I told you."

"No. You said you had a hunch but didn't know for sure until I told you. Why the hunch?"

"One of the guys on our team heard about him and told me. Simple as that."

Jerry pushed off the chair. Fred stopped him. "Okay. It was Manning."

Gunter opened an eye.

"What does Manning have to do with any of this?"

Fred crossed one leg over the other. "Everything

and nothing."

Jerry wanted to tell the man that was his line but remained silent, allowing Fred to continue.

"There was this case in Connecticut. A missing child. We were desperate to find her, only no one could. We wanted to make sure we would be able to make a difference in the future, so we sent one of our guys, Hal, to North Carolina to visit with an expert on tracking dogs."

"Mike Craig of Public Safety Dogs Inc."

Fred nodded. "That's the guy. Anyway, it just so happened that Hal was there at the same time Manning was coming in to train with his new dog, and they bumped into each other."

At the mention of Manning's other dog, Gunter growled a deep growl.

"They ran into each other in the bar later that night. He and Hal start talking, and Hal tells him the reason he's there. He tells about the kid and how she's most likely dead. Manning pipes up and tells how his dog would be able to find her. Hal assures him they did everything they could, to which Manning, having had a bit too much to drink, says it would take a ghost to find a ghost. He goes on to tell how his dog is now a ghost and crying in his beer because the dog would rather be with you than him."

Gunter yawned a squeaky yawn.

Jerry shook his head. "The dog is with me because his former owner is a loose cannon. That guy is going to get someone killed."

Gunter groaned and rolled over in the other direction.

"And you think you're a better fit for the dog?"

Jerry looked at the bed. "I do."

"Why's that?"

A million reasons rolled around in Jerry's head. In the end, he only had one answer. "Because we need each other."

A thud sounded. Jerry looked to see Gunter's tail thumping the bed. Jerry turned his attention back to Fred. "This Hal guy. He's in the habit of listening to ghost stories?"

"Our men, myself included, are in the habit of being able to decipher the truth. You've been around the world. Surely you can agree that most rumors are based on some shred of fact. Besides, it was a small town. Hal found the guy's story entertaining."

"So what finally convinced him the story had teeth?"

Fred reached across the table and picked up his cell phone. He thumbed through it for several seconds before turning it around for Jerry to see the article in the Louisville newspaper, with a picture of Jerry standing beside a zombie dog. "Interesting article, don't you think?"

Jerry rolled his neck.

"Only Manning was adamant that dog wasn't pretending to be a zombie. He made quite the scene of it, pulling out photos of his former partner and making Hal compare the two. That torn ear was a bit too much to overlook. You hit our radar, and shortly after we started looking into you, you started uncovering dead bodies."

Jerry stretched and intertwined his fingers behind his head. "Technically, I don't uncover them."

"That's right. You just point people in the right direction. Why is that?"

Jerry shrugged. "I'm not in this for the limelight."

Fred laughed and held up his phone. "And yet there you are on the front cover of the *Courier-Journal*."

"That was the dog's idea."

"Do you make a habit of listening to that dog?"

"Does the job offer depend on the right answer?"

Fred uncrossed his legs and leaned forward in his chair. "Does that mean you're accepting our offer?"

"I'll think about it." Jerry stood, and Gunter jumped down from the bed. Jerry reached for the doorknob and hesitated. "This case with the missing kid. Who is she to you?"

Fred's head snapped up. He looked at Jerry for a full moment before answering. "My niece."

"You ever find her?"

"No. We have a suspect. But he's walking free, as we've never been able to fully link him to the case."

Jerry studied the man and knew he was telling the truth. "Connecticut is on my way. Send me the address, and I'll see what I can do."

Fred's shoulders dropped and his lips trembled as he reached for his phone.

***

Jerry stood in front of the window, staring out at the parking lot, mulling over the events of the last couple of days. He pulled his cell phone from his pocket and dialed Seltzer's number.

"Jerry, my boy, June and I were just talking about you. She's home. I was telling her about our adventure."

"Which one?"

"Go on inside, and I'll be in shortly." Seltzer grew quiet for a moment and Jerry knew he was waiting for his wife to leave. A door closed in the distance. "Okay, I can talk. I tried to get hold of you earlier. You had me worried."

"No need. I've got everything under control."

"Everything?"

I sure hope so. "Seems to be."

"Fabel?"

"We had a chat." The guy was a loose cannon, to be sure. But he was committed to family and Jerry felt he had reached him on that level.

"And?"

Jerry laughed. "He made me an offer I couldn't

refuse."

"Quit beating around the bush and tell me."

"He offered me a million dollars to hand him the killer."

"You caught the killer?"

"No. But Fabel's willing to wait."

"So you agreed to his offer?"

"What do you think?" That Seltzer even thought he would consider it hurt.

"I don't see you going along with it, but you're still alive, so you must have made some kind of deal."

"I told him what happened to the man after he is in prison is out of my control."

"You know they'll probably put him in solitary confinement."

"We'll see." Therein lay the problem. Even though Jerry had found Rosie, he wasn't any closer than he'd been the day before. Jerry rolled his neck. "I got a job offer today."

"Did you take it?"

"I'm thinking about it." The truth was the offer had a lot of draws, especially the part that took Seltzer off the hook.

"I didn't know you were looking."

"I wasn't. It found me." *Just like everything else in my life*. Jerry laughed to himself.

"Must be good if you're actually considering it."

"Let's just say I had two offers I couldn't refuse

today, and this is the better of the two."

Seltzer blew out a low whistle. "Better than a million dollars?"

"Better than two million. Fabel doubled it when I refused." The thing was Jerry thought Fabel would have agreed to just about any price if Jerry had been willing to negotiate. "Hey, remember those two suits I was telling you about?"

"Yep. I still haven't found anything about them."

"Don't bother. We had a little chat." As they spoke, Jerry felt the beginning of a tingle. "Turns out their names really are Fred and Barney."

"You don't say?"

"Yep."

"Did you ever find out how they knew about the dog?"

"They didn't. Not until I admitted it." Jerry looked over at Gunter and sighed. "Seems my poker face isn't as good as I thought."

"I don't get it. How could they have known in the first place?"

"Manning told them." Jerry closed his eyes, picturing the man.

"My Manning?"

"One and the same. Turns out he saw that photo of me and Gunter. Long story short – he shot off at the mouth to someone who actually took time to listen to the man."

"Is it going to be a problem?"

"Nope." *At least not with the secret handshake club.*

"How can you be so sure?"

"It's what I do. Remember?" Gunter barked and jumped up, placing his paws on the windowsill. He looked toward the parking lot and continued barking at something Jerry couldn't see. Jerry looked closer and saw a shadow move in front of his Durango. "Hey, Fabel promised to call off his goons. You and June are safe."

"You believe him?"

"For now." Gunter began pawing at the glass. Jerry placed a hand on the dog's shoulders to settle him.

"Good to know."

"Listen, I've got some things to take care of before I head out."

"Anything exciting?"

"Just a little sightseeing."

"Then where are you off to?"

"Connecticut. Promised Fred I'd look into a missing person case for him. I'll fill you in along the way. Listen, I think the dog needs to go out." Jerry didn't bother reminding the man that Gunter was a ghost and could go out on his own. Jerry ended the call and Gunter reacted with eager circles. "Come on, dog, let's go see what the trouble is."

***

Rosie was sitting in the passenger seat of the

Durango when Jerry approached. Jerry walked around and opened the door for Gunter, who jumped in and made his way to the back seat. Jerry noticed a woman walking a tiny poodle as he climbed inside the driver's seat. Gunter barked and stuck his head out the glass. Jerry shushed the dog and turned his attention to Rosie. "You looking for a ride?"

"Yes. But only to the city center. I'm staying here."

"I take it you spoke with the others?"

"Yes, they voted and said I can stay. They even gave me my own job."

"You mean we have to work after we die?"

"This really isn't work. It's more like play. But I want to show you."

***

Jerry went to the kiosk and purchased a ticket for the ghost walk – something that went against his nature since he usually didn't have to pay to see ghosts. Still, Rosie was excited to show him her new "life," and since he felt somewhat responsible for the transition, he wanted to see how things turned out.

The woman giving the tour was middle-aged and dressed for the part in black from head to foot. Thus far, she hadn't claimed to have actually seen any of the ghosts she was telling them about. They stopped at a two-story dark grey house, and the group of nearly a dozen moved in close in order to hear the woman's words. Not wishing to spoil the others' fun with his eye-rolling, Jerry stayed near the back of the procession.

"Do you think we'll see any ghosts today?" someone in the crowd whispered. Gunter moved through the small group, sidled up in front of the woman, and wagged his tail. The woman didn't notice. Gunter lowered his tail and made his way back to Jerry, leaning his body against the side of Jerry's leg.

They'd visited several sites where ghosts were supposed to be without seeing anything. Even Jerry found himself disappointed, as some of the stories were rather interesting. It didn't mean there were no ghosts where the woman claimed them to be. It just meant said spirits weren't in the mood to be seen. As they approached a cream-colored house similar in structure to where they'd begun their tour, the guide started her tale. As she spoke of the unusual happenings that had occurred there of late, the curtain in the upstairs room moved, and a shadow passed from one side of the window to the other.

Several in the crowd gasped, making Jerry realize he wasn't the only one to see it. The tour guide's mouth gaped open as she strained to see what the others were describing. As she did, Rosie appeared at the woman's side.

Plopping her finger into her mouth, Rosie pulled it out and stuck it into the woman's left ear.

Though he wasn't in a position to see the tour

guide's face, Jerry watched as the woman battled the unseen intrusion.

Rosie giggled in childish delight as she weaved in and between the visitors, brushing a bit too close to some and whispering in the ears of others. A man stood next to his wife, scowling at the claims of others who were excitedly telling of feeling a spirit among them. Rosie produced a feather, which she waved under the man's nose until he sneezed.

As the group moved on, Rosie dropped to her knees, scratching Gunter behind the ear. The dog leaned into her touch, and Jerry waited for them to say their goodbyes.

Giving one last head scratch, Rosie stood and faced him. "Thank you."

"Just doing my job. Speaking of which, this is a good fit for you."

Rosie bobbed her head and smiled. "It was Corney's idea. I think it was his way of keeping me away from the waterfront. He never liked me going there."

Something told Jerry the fellow wasn't going to enjoy being called Corney either. He refrained from saying as much. Some things were better left worked out for themselves. "I'm going to get the guy who did this. I promise not to stop until I do."

Gunter gave a woof. Jerry looked to see another tour heading in their direction. "Looks like you're on."

Rosie leaned in and kissed Jerry on the cheek. She turned her head ever so slightly and whispered into the wind. As she did, the number 207 came to mind. A chill ran the length of his spine. He opened his mouth to ask what it meant and Rosie touched her finger to his lips to silence him. "I'm not allowed to tell you any more."

Rosie withdrew her hand, waved her fingers and disappeared with the breeze. A second later, she appeared in the same window as she had before. She lifted her hand and blew him a kiss, and he knew that she was saying goodbye.

***

Jerry paced the length of room 207 for at least the hundredth time. He'd been retracing his route for at least twenty minutes, yet nothing about the room called to him. Two-oh-seven might have meaning, but not within this room. Gunter crouched on the bed, hip tilted to the side, watching Jerry's every move. That the dog was relaxed told him all he needed to know. Their work here was done and it was time to move on.

Join Jerry McNeal and his ghostly K-9 partner as they put their gifts to good use!

Now available for preorder:

Mystic Angel – book 8 in The Jerry McNeal Series
https://www.amazon.com/ dp/B0B5YMK948

And, coming Spring of 2023, join Jerry and Gunter as they travel to Deadwood to see Jonesy and a lively cast of spirits in *Spirit of Deadwood*, a fun-filled, full-length Jerry McNeal novel.
https://www.amazon.com/dp/B0B1C9XKX7

About the Author

Sherry A. Burton writes in multiple genres and has won numerous awards for her books. Sherry's awards include the coveted Charles Loring Brace Award for historical accuracy within her historical fiction series, The Orphan Train Saga. Sherry is a member of the National Orphan Train Society, presents lectures on the history of the orphan trains, and is listed on the NOTC Speaker's Bureau as an approved speaker.

Originally from Kentucky, Sherry and her Retired Navy Husband now call Michigan home. Sherry enjoys traveling and spending time with her husband of more than forty years.

Made in the USA
Monee, IL
12 August 2022